THE LATIMER MERCY

Robert Richardson was born in Manchester in 1940. Since 1960 he has been a journalist, working for many years on the *Daily Mail* and contributing to, among others, the *Independent*, the *Guardian* and the *Sunday Times*. He is married with two sons and lives in Old Hatfield. Robert Richardson is also the author of *Bellringer Street*, *The Book of the Dead*, *The Dying of the Light*, *Sleeping in the Blood* and *The Lazarus Tree*; all of which are published by Gollancz.

Also by Robert Richardson in Gollancz Crime

BELLRINGER STREET
THE BOOK OF THE DEAD
THE DYING OF THE LIGHT
SLEEPING IN THE BLOOD

THE LATIMER MERCY

by

Robert Richardson

GOLLANCZ CRIME

Gollancz Crime is an imprint of Victor Gollancz Ltd
14 Henrietta Street, London WC2E 8QJ

First published in Great Britain 1985
by Victor Gollancz Ltd

First Gollancz Crime edition 1989
Second impression October 1992

A catalogue record for this book
is available from the British Library

ISBN 0-575-04537-X

Printed and bound in Great Britain
by Cox & Wyman Ltd, Reading

To my Mother

AUTHOR'S NOTE

That St Albans exists is beyond dispute; that
Vercaster bears a marked resemblance to that
city is acknowledged; that the characters and
incidents of this book are imaginary is certain.

THE LATIMER MERCY

Chapter 1

"REBECCA, MY DEAR," said Augustus Maltravers, "you are a child to make one contemplate the possible attractions of celibacy."

This reasonably well turned aphorism, which he had spent some minutes mentally constructing, was totally ignored by his three-year-old niece who contentedly continued to dismantle his retractable ball-point pen which had proved a greater attraction than a scattered and rejected collection of ingenious toys marrying education with entertainment. There was a slight twang as the spring jumped out, much to her delight, and, quite inexplicably, a further streak of ink appeared on her hand; the exit of the spring appeared to trigger a total self-destruct mechanism and the entire pen collapsed into its component parts. Her mother, Melissa, came back into the kitchen, instantly comprehended the scene and took appropriate action. In a single maternal movement she scooped Rebecca up with one arm, planted her in the middle of a previously demolished yellow plastic construction and stepped expertly through the various pieces of debris to the sink.

"Don't give her things like pens, Augustus," she said. "At this age everything ends up in the mouth."

Maltravers retrieved what he hoped were all the dismembered parts and began the formidable task of reassembly in the proper order. His wife, with whom he had shared a physically satisfactory but otherwise hollow brief marriage, had once remarked that he only just understood the principle of the hammer and that he approached anything more technical than replacing a light bulb with caution and a profound sense of the hostility of the inanimate.

"Isn't it time to go and collect Diana?" asked Melissa, and

Maltravers realised from her tone of dissolving patience that he had failed to fulfil the role of avuncular child-minder as surely as he would never make a manufacturer of pens.

"She's not due for nearly an hour," he countered cautiously.

Melissa's back made subtle but eloquent movements plainly indicating that that was not the required response and Rebecca's coincidental demands of a lavatorial nature convinced him that his departure would be prudent. Like all people without children, he found their basic natural functions threatening.

"I'll wander round to the cathedral," he said.

"What an excellent idea. Oh, and you can buy some avocados while you're out. They're for dinner before we go tonight."

Suitably instructed on the correct methods of assessing avocados, Maltravers set off into the streets of Vercaster. As a residentiary cathedral canon, his brother-in-law Michael occupied a handsome, if tied, Georgian house in the cathedral precincts of Punt Yard, conveniently central but constantly plagued by the cars of tourists and shoppers. The only possibility of punting lay on the lethargic waters of the River Verta, nearly a quarter of a mile away in the hollow of the valley which the cathedral and its compact city had once dominated; before, that is, late Victorian development brought by the railways, and the questionable pleasure of commuting the twenty miles or so into London, had spread the stain of urban growth about the adjacent land.

What Maltravers irreverently — and to Michael's mild annoyance — referred to as God's desirable detached property loomed to his left as he stepped through the front door, the end of the Lady Chapel almost opposite him. Vercaster Cathedral owed its existence to a Saxon peasant girl, its splendour to sheep and its survival to tobacco. Etheldreda, an otherwise unremarkable child, had fallen into a transported fit one day on the hill where it now stood, crying that she could see hosts of angels and hear the sound of bells. Shortly afterwards, she died in a similar state of ecstasy and the contemporary authorities, with an eye to their vulnerable immortal souls, had erected the first church on the site of her experience. The Normans had developed the building but their work had been gloriously overtaken in the fourteenth

8

century when Flemish immigrants, combining their weaving skills with the abundant supply of wool, created vast local wealth coinciding with the soaring burst of Perpendicular architecture. The result was an ascending masterpiece of Man praising God in stone and stained glass, with the particular magnificence of the Chapter House by the south transept. Its incredibly delicate stone tracery cascaded in a dome of lace-like interlocking triangles of woven masonry above eight burning windows of polychromatic glass. After the Benedictine monks had been summarily evicted to provide Henry VIII with some much-needed cash, the structure had declined until the early nineteenth century when one Thomas Reade, a son of the city who had made his fortune in the plantations of Virginia, had paid for its complete and intelligent restoration, saving it from the later ham-fisted attentions of the Victorians.

Architecturally it was marred only by an external folly, the hundred and forty foot tower at the west end whose height had been increased in 1620 to make it theoretically visible throughout the diocese. The additional weight thus imposed had caused dramatic but inelegant flying buttresses to become necessary at its base. The whole enterprise had suffered an unfortunate start when the aging Bishop who was to dedicate the extension collapsed and died while climbing the additional stairs. He had been granted the post mortem compensation of having the entire tower named after him and in distant parts of the diocese the rhyming couplet

> When Talbot's Tower's by morning seen
> Then rain will come before the e'en

had formed part of local weather lore ever since with its alternative,

> When Talbot's Tower you cannot see
> It's raining cats and dogs on thee

completing the inevitable meteorological logic of such phenomena.

Maltravers turned left out of the house, away from the main road at the opposite end of Punt Yard, and followed the silhouette of his shadow towards the south transept door. He was a tall, angular man whose movements fell just short of clumsiness. Beneath erratic brown hair was a long face which seemed to have lived only the summers of his thirty-four years; what had been irritatingly youthful features ten years earlier were becoming increasingly advantageous with the passage of time. He was in Vercaster for the city's resurrected Arts Festival, an event originally started to celebrate Victoria's Diamond Jubilee but which had gone into a marked decline and eventual death after being left during the 1930s in the care of an elderly citizen whose exclusive passion for pastoral dance had first limited, then totally suffocated, its appeal. It had now been reborn to mark the 400th anniversary of a visit by Elizabeth I to grant the city's charter. The cost of feeding her camp-followers had regrettably bankrupted the first Earl of Verta; happily for the family his great-grandson had restored their fortunes after the Restoration by prudently supplying his sister as a mistress to Charles II.

Arrangements augured well for the reborn festival. A respectable string quartet, symphony orchestra and jazz composer of whom even the Bishop had heard, were to perform; a poet with some claim to rival Larkin was to give a reading; the not unaccomplished Vercaster Players' amateur dramatic society had dusted off and adapted the city's ancient Mystery Plays cycle, which had lain dormant for more than a century, and other sundry local artistic talents were to add to a fortnight of general activity. The climax was to be a Medieval fair on the long green slope that ran down from the cathedral to the river, with the final Mystery Plays being performed in the evening and fireworks to bring the whole affair to what it was hoped would be a satisfactory conclusion.

Maltravers was involved that first Saturday evening, following a request from his sister who was on the organising committee. About a year previously he had had a trilogy of plays called *Success City* put on by Channel 4 with a hitherto unknown actress called Diana Porter in the lead. While critically successful, the plays had not posed any threat to the audience figures enjoyed by endless narratives of life in the North of England or South of

Texas, and Diana had been quite happy to accept an invitation to put on a one-woman show in Vercaster. Thereafter things took an unexpected turn when she appeared in an iconoclastic production of *Hedda Gabler*, including a full-frontal nude scene which Ibsen had inexplicably overlooked. This experimental and obscure theatrical event might have passed unnoticed had not a Fleet Street paper of flimsy content but ludicrously high sales obtained a picture of the scene and published it under the words "Hedda Liner!" in the size of type one would have anticipated them reserving for an elopement from the Vatican.

Several million readers, previously unaware of Mrs Gabler, Mr Ibsen and even the general location of Norway, were briefly titillated and Diana became the legitimate target for gossip columnists and news editors looking for a new personality to pursue in the interests of a free Press. She accepted the benefits of such abundant publicity with cynical amusement and exploited them to some considerable financial advantage; she could rely on her acting talent to carry her through once the silliness had passed.

The *Vercaster Times*, while acting with restraint as a local paper in a polite cathedral city and not actually publishing the notorious photograph, drew attention to Diana's proposed appearance at the festival, causing murmurs of discontent in civic and clerical circles. Matters were redeemed, however, when she appeared in a Sunday evening religious television programme, reading extracts from the works of Julian of Norwich with intelligence and impeccable taste, wearing a demure and becoming dress not dissimilar to one owned by the Bishop's wife. A further performance in a "traditional" — Old Vic circa 1936 — production of *Macbeth* attracted critical approval in papers with smaller circulations but of the quality to be found in clergymen's households. Having established there would be no repetition of the Gabler incident in Vercaster, the popular press went off to be a nuisance somewhere else and the festival was able to benefit from a more acceptable level of publicity. Melissa, originally appalled, was delighted and awarded Maltravers the ultimate household accolade of a hero biscuit.

As Maltravers approached the south transept he observed a

new addition to the local scenery in the shape of a uniformed policeman standing outside the door. The presence of the constabulary, or their fellow conspirators the traffic wardens, was not uncommon in Punt Yard where the love of God took second place to the carved tablets of parking restrictions, but clearly this representative of law and order was performing some manner of guard duty.

"Good morning," Maltravers said cheerfully as he reached him.

"Good morning, sir. I'm afraid that if you have business in the cathedral you can't go in."

Maltravers raised an eyebrow. "My business might be going in to pray."

Clearly uncertain as to the powers of secular authority with regard to the obstruction of such a blameless activity, the officer was caught off balance and looked uncomfortable.

"Yes, sir. Well . . . I'm afraid there's been a bit of trouble," he said.

"Trouble? What sort? Human sacrifice? Black Mass at the High Altar? Surely not naked nuns?"

The policeman felt he was being mocked in the course of his duty which, while falling short of actual interference, was still to be deplored.

"I'm very sorry, but I can't allow you to go in," he said stiffly, having noticeably dropped the "sir" from his address.

"But I do have a rather important appointment with Canon Cowan," said Maltravers. "It's in connection with the festival." This was totally untrue but his curiosity had been aroused and he was determined to gain entry. "Is it just this door that's cut off?" He had correctly assumed that it was unlikely that all the entrances to the cathedral would have their own separate uniformed guardians.

"Canon Cowan is with Detective Sergeant Jackson," the policeman replied, with the obvious feeling that he had played an untrumpable ace of argument.

"Then he'll certainly want to see me. I'm his solicitor." Having started lying Maltravers could see no reason for not carrying mendacity as far as necessary.

12

"I don't think it's a matter that . . ." began the policeman but Maltravers became unnervingly authoritative.

"I must be the judge of that," he snapped and walked swiftly round the obstacle and straight through the door reflecting that when the young constable later discovered that he had been outmanoeuvred he could use the experience to future benefit.

He strode through the transept, past the tourists' shop and bookstall, without having any idea where Michael and the law might be. Almost immediately he saw them standing to his left by the north wall of the nave, in front of a small display case with a flat glass top which stood near the organ. The Detective Sergeant, broad shouldered and with a thick brown moustache, was writing in a notebook as Maltravers reached them.

"What exactly was it called, sir?" he was asking.

"The Latimer Mercy," Michael replied. Maltravers looked at the empty display case.

"The Latimer Mercy?" he echoed. "What's happened to it?"

"It's been stolen," said Michael.

"That," said Maltravers, "is offensive."

"We call it criminal, sir," said the detective. "I'm sorry, I don't know who this gentleman is."

"Oh, it's my brother-in-law, Mr Maltravers," explained Michael. "The writer. He's here for the festival."

"I see, sir," said Jackson. "Now, you were saying, sir, that it's the Latimer Mercy. What exactly is that?"

"Well, it's . . . you must be new to Vercaster."

"I joined this force from Lincolnshire a month ago," Jackson replied patiently. "I assume that if I'd been here longer I would know all about the Latimer Mercy."

"Well, it's a considerable treasure of the cathedral. How can I explain? Have you heard of the Merry Bibles?"

"No, sir. Is that something else I should know?"

"No, but you probably would know if . . ." Michael, who was excellent at addressing the captive audience of a congregation with a prepared sermon, found question and answer situations trying. "Augustus, perhaps you . . . ?"

"The Merry Bibles were a misprinted version of 1546," Maltravers explained briskly. "They were printed in Vercaster and

13

many were destroyed after the error was noticed. It was in Psalm 25, verse 10, where it read 'All the paths of the Lord are merry and truth unto such as keep his covenant and his testimonies'. Frankly, I think it gains something through the mistake."

"And so this was a Merry Bible?" said Jackson, indicating the empty case.

"Yes, but a very special one. In this edition the misprint had been corrected with the word 'merry' crossed out and 'mercy' written in the margin with the initials 'HL' alongside it. The legend is that the correction was made by Bishop Hugh Latimer, hence the Latimer Mercy."

Jackson's next question was surprising. "When was it done?" he asked.

"That's difficult to say," Michael put in. "It was presumably here last night and the theft was . . ."

"No, I don't mean that. When was the correction made?"

Michael looked confused both by the nature of the question and the fact that it was made. "I don't think anybody knows. Augustus?"

"I couldn't even guess." Maltravers looked keenly at Jackson. "But I'm interested in why you should ask."

"It's just that Latimer preached in my home town of Stamford in 1550 — November, I think — and he could obviously have passed through here on his way." Jackson smiled slyly at Maltravers before speaking to Michael. "I imagine I'll learn things like that about Vercaster when I've been here a little longer."

Michael, who found criticism, however subtly put, disquieting, looked slightly annoyed, but Maltravers returned Jackson's smile with a grin of admiration.

"*Touché*, sergeant," he said. "And your theory's interesting as well. However, this is a very disturbing affair for the cathedral."

"Of course," Jackson replied, recognising he could communicate better with Maltravers. "What would be the value of the Bible?"

Maltravers pulled a face. "I'm no great expert, but any Bible before about 1580 would fetch a fair price. A Coverdale of 1535 brought thirty thousand dollars in New York a couple of years

14

ago, although a Matthews Bible of 1537 brought only six thousand the same year. The Latimer Mercy was rebound in the last century, which would greatly diminish its worth."

"What effect would the misprint have?" Jackson asked.

"On its value not a great deal," said Maltravers. "People think they're going to retire when they come across a Breeches Bible, but that was published, with one or more editions a year, over thirty years. On the other hand, the correction makes the Latimer Mercy unique. It's not just going to crop up at Sotheby's or Christie's."

Jackson nodded then lifted the lid of the case, which Maltravers could see had been forced open with a screwdriver or similar instrument.

"You didn't protect it very well, sir," he commented.

Michael looked uncomfortable. "We have a somewhat radical Dean who feels excessive security has no place in the church," he explained. "If he had his way, I imagine he would leave the entire building unlocked day and night."

"I think you'd find we'd disapprove of that. The average villain isn't noted for his piety." Jackson sniffed and closed the lid. "Very well. On the face of it, we may assume it was taken for, or by, a specific person. When did you discover it was missing?"

"About ten o'clock this morning. One of the ladies who serves in the tourists' shop noticed it. As far as we know, it was there last night."

"And the cathedral was locked overnight?"

"Certainly," said Michael, making it clear he did not approve of the Dean's open-house preferences.

"No sign of a break-in to the building?"

"Not as far as I'm aware."

"An inside job," put in Maltravers adding an unnecessary note of drama to his voice. Jackson smiled seriously.

"Possibly," he said in the tone of a professional being patient with an amateur. "What time does the cathedral close in the evening?"

"About eight o'clock at this time of year."

Jackson's next questions were thoughts spoken aloud. "So, possibly late in the evening . . . nobody would have specifically

15

checked? No . . . or this morning after the cathedral opened . . . or during the night." He paused for a moment, thinking silently.

"Very well. We'll need to talk to everyone who has a key for any of the doors."

Michael looked horrified. "But some of them are very senior clergy," he protested. "You're surely not suggesting . . ."

"Everyone who has a key," said Jackson impassively. "Perhaps one has been stolen," he added, to defuse Michael's indignation. "We'll also want to talk to all the staff who work in the cathedral. They might have seen something suspicious. You have guides?"

"There are no guided tours as such, except for parties who make their own arrangements," said Michael. "But there are a number of people who walk around the building and explain things to visitors."

"Are they told to keep an eye out for anything untoward?"

"They're not formally told, but I'm sure they understand that they should."

"Right," Jackson closed his notebook and slipped it into his pocket. "You have a rota showing who was on duty yesterday afternoon and this morning?"

"Yes," said Michael. "It's on a notice-board in the shop. I'll show you." All three of them turned back towards the south transept.

"Of course," said Maltravers. "Any suggestion as to the motive would be a great help."

"Yes, sir," said Jackson. "But lacking any definite evidence, that's a matter for speculation. In the meantime, we'll have to follow the usual channels of inquiry."

Jackson collected the constable who was still standing guard at the transept door and told him to take the names from the guides' rota list. A small, slightly globular man carrying a small case walked in and joined them.

"Morning," he said. "Higson. Fingerprints. Where?" Long sentences were clearly not his habit.

"Just round that corner," said Jackson, pointing. "Wooden case on the left. You can't miss it." Higson, without further expenditure of words, walked briskly on.

16

"I would have thought that case would have been smothered in fingerprints," said Maltravers helpfully. "People have a habit of poking at such things."

"Procedures," Jackson said briefly. "We'll need a statement from you as well, Canon Cowan. Perhaps you could come to the station later today?"

"Well, yes, although I don't know that I can . . ."

"And of course the person who first discovered the theft," Jackson interrupted. "Is she still here?"

"No, she was rather upset by the incident and I sent her home."

"Well, we don't need to trouble her immediately, but perhaps you could bring her down when you come later."

"Yes, of course," agreed Michael, as legal authority overcame ecclesiastical dignity. "After lunch?"

"Thank you, sir, that will be fine. Just ask to see me when you arrive. Mr Maltravers." With a brief nod Jackson departed.

"I must go and tell the Dean what has happened," said Michael. "What did you want anyway?"

"Nothing, I was just passing the time," Maltravers replied. "Diana and Tess are due in about an hour and I'm going to collect them."

"Oh. Yes, of course." The imminent arrival of expected guests seemed to take on the proportions of great misfortune for Michael with common larceny breaking out on hallowed ground. "I'll see you all at lunch."

After he left, Maltravers walked back to where the taciturn Higson was performing the mysteries of his art on the empty display case and watched him thoughtfully. His instant reaction of feeling offended was still with him; while he quite regularly disputed accepted religious beliefs, he respected anything enriched by antiquity and found the traditions of the church in language, architecture, ceremony and behaviour, attractive. The Latimer Mercy had been printed in Henry VIII's final infected years and corrected — if Jackson's interesting theory was correct — before Spenser, Marlowe or Shakespeare were born, and possibly by the man whose ringing words of certainty as the flames ate his body five years later, were a clarion call of faith

17

triumphant which Maltravers could not share but did respect. It belonged to no man because it belonged to all men and its removal dismayed him; putting aside all other considerations, it was a book and to Maltravers a book was a holy thing. But why, he reflected, had it been taken? He had an uneasy feeling that the motive was sinister.

The same thought, but this time as only one among several possibilities, was going through the mind of David Jackson as he drove the short distance back to Vercaster's main police station, his mind revolving about what had happened and what had to be done. Check with county headquarters to see if the theft fitted an established pattern of crimes; extend inquiries to other police forces for the same thing. But this was a very specific theft, probably with a customer waiting. All air and sea ports would have to be alerted and Customs told to watch for it. On balance, it was probably going out of the country so Interpol would need to be informed. It was an odd one. Petty theft and major bank robberies shared common factors of recognisable greed, following obvious patterns which made up nearly all of police work. Anything that would not fit the norm had its own unique reasons behind it, and there lay difficulties. Jackson's great virtue as a detective was that he kept his mind open; the wealthy secret collector was one obvious theory but was there something else? Strange crimes, he reflected, were done by or for strange people for unknown and very personal motives. How strange and how personal was impossible to fathom and in such darkness anything might lie.

Chapter 2

CLUTCHING A BAG of what he hoped were satisfactory avocados, Maltravers watched one of the regular London trains draw into Vercaster station, quite certain that, by the mysterious laws which govern such things, he was standing on that part of the platform farthest removed from the carriage out of which Tess and Diana would alight. In a changing and unreliable world, he was reassured to discover that he was right when two figures appeared as far north along the platform as he was standing to the south.

Tess, he observed as he walked towards them, was wearing an unaccustomed hat, presumably because of memories from her childhood when for a woman to enter a church with her head uncovered brought sidelong glances which were the metaphorical equivalent of being stoned as an adulteress. Her relationship with Maltravers went back to a dinner party where a well-meaning hostess had thoughtfully paired them off individually with two other people and had been quite upset to discover that her ability to read personalities was appalling. Like Diana, Tess was also an actress, but without the innate flair or inclination for fortuitous publicity; she looked rather like Billie Whitelaw. Diana, carrying with difficulty a suitcase of amazing proportions for an overnight stay, was dressed as A Well Known Personality if not Actually A Star, in a purple billowing dress with her long blonde hair looking as casual as only great expense and trouble could make it.

"Augustus, darling!" she cried excessively. "Have you been waiting awfully long?"

"Stop playing the grande dame, silly woman," Maltravers replied equably. "They've got more sense in the provinces."

"Sorry." And the Diana Porter Maltravers had great faith in immediately surfaced. "God, I've got to learn to stop it."

19

"And you'd better stop saying 'God' as well. The company you'll be keeping doesn't throw Him around so casually."

"I shall be pious and pure as a nun."

"That," said Maltravers, kissing her briefly on the cheek and stepping round her to greet Tess, "will be a remarkable performance even by your standards."

He took Tess's case and Diana's modest portmanteau and staggered ludicrously for a few paces.

"Thank God it's only a one-woman show," he remarked.

"Now you've said it," said Diana accusingly.

"What? Oh, God. Yes, well it doesn't matter with me. There's a general feeling that I'm beyond redemption anyway. But you have a reputation to live down."

In the taxi back to Punt Yard, Maltravers told them about the Latimer Mercy theft.

"What a senseless thing," said Tess.

"That's how it appears, but I think there may be a very strange sense behind it," Maltravers replied.

"What do you mean?"

"It's so pointless, there has to be a point," he said. "It can't be sold, so why steal it?"

"Obviously some eccentric wants to keep it in his private collection and pore over it in secret."

"Then may his soul and his progeny rot," said Maltravers fiercely. "He'd be the sort of specimen who would make me want to believe there really is a Hell."

"It worries you, doesn't it?" said Tess.

"It . . . offends me." Maltravers used the word again with growing layers of feeling behind it. "And, yes, it worries me in a way. Putting aside the nutty collector theory, I find it . . . disturbing."

Diana, whose affection for and knowledge of Maltravers fell only just short of Tess's, was equally sensitive to his feelings and changed the conversation to the festival as they completed their journey.

Melissa, with the miraculous gifts of a housewife, had transformed her home from the semi-disaster zone Maltravers had left earlier into neatness commensurate with its Georgian elegance, reassembled Rebecca into a presentable infant and herself into a Canon's wife.

"Hello, you must be Diana," she said as she opened the front door. "Come in and I'll show you your room and you can change." With businesslike hospitality, Diana was escorted upstairs. "Hello, Tess," Melissa called backwards. "Augustus will look after you."

Tess watched Melissa disappear upstairs. "Your sister still doesn't approve of me," she remarked.

"She disapproves of us both," said Maltravers. "Divorce is regarded in clerical households as contrary to the Almighty's scheme of things and adultery is generally frowned upon. We are in separate rooms."

"Separate rooms, for God's sake!"

"Not so loud. They are next to each other — and Melissa arranged that."

Tess gave a ladylike grunt of grudging approval.

"I expect there's grace at mealtimes," she added as a final sideswipe.

"Yes. And in any man's house I will respect his feelings."

"Don't be pompous. Let's go upstairs and . . ."

"Enough, woman!" shouted Maltravers. "There is a child in the house."

Rebecca, the child in the house, was the catalyst of an unexpected revelation. Diana, whom Maltravers had never associated with children, sat on the floor with her, full of genuine interest and Rebecca, clearly deciding that anyone who looked like a fairytale princess was to be instantly trusted, responded at once. While Melissa completed the preparations for lunch, Maltravers and Tess observed the pair of them with amazement until Michael returned.

"At this point in the play, a cleric enters the room," said Maltravers as he did so. "He looks concerned."

"Good morning, Tess," said Michael, ignoring him. "And I presume this is . . . ?"

"Oh, hello. I'm sorry I can't get up but, as you see, I'm rather busy," said Diana from the floor.

"This is not a role I expected you to play," said Maltravers.

"No, not many people do," Diana replied with an odd smile and returned all her attention to Rebecca.

"And how did the Dean take the news?" Maltravers asked Michael.

"Very badly. He does not want the church highly protected because he feels it does not finally matter if anything is taken . . ."

"After all, you can't steal God," Maltravers put in.

"Quite. But he's still shocked when something disappears, particularly if it's one of the cathedral's treasures. Anyway, we'd better have lunch. I have to see the police with Miss Targett."

"You're joking!" Maltravers laughed.

"Of course I'm not. You were with me when that man Jackson asked us to go."

"No, no, no. I mean there isn't really someone called Miss Targett is there?"

"To make matters worse," said Melissa entering the room, "there are two of them. The Misses Targett. Come on through, lunch is ready."

Over a collection of cheeses, cold meats and salad, conversation turned to Diana's performance in the evening. It was to be held in the Chapter House and was called "The Cross on the Circle". Maltravers and Diana refused to be drawn when they were asked what the title meant.

"You'll have to wait and see," Maltravers said.

"I would have thought it was fairly obvious," said Michael, fishing fastidiously in the remains of the salad. "The circle is the world and the cross is Christianity on top of it."

"A most shrewd interpretation," said Maltravers, keeping his face immobile and Diana kicked his ankle under the table, just as the meal was interrupted by the sound of the doorbell.

"That will be Miss Targett," said Michael glancing at the clock.

"She whom I must meet," said Maltravers. "I'll go, and I promise to restrain myself."

When he opened the door a young and concerned looking clergyman stood on the step.

"Not Miss Targett, I presume?" said Maltravers.

The cleric's face gave a twitch of bewilderment. "I beg your pardon?"

"I'm sorry. We were expecting someone else. You obviously want to see Canon Cowan."

"If it's convenient," said the young man. "I'm sorry to arrive unexpectedly, but . . ."

"Not at all, although I'm afraid he's going out shortly." Maltravers pulled the door fully open. "Please come in and I'll let him know you're here."

The visitor's immediately obvious concern had rapidly transmuted into positive distress. Maltravers noticed the nervous trembling of his fingers; his face, which had clearly never known plumpness, became increasingly unsettled. He ran a hasty, agitated hand across his neatly-cut black hair and seemed uncertain what to do.

"Oh, if he's going out . . . I don't wish to . . . I'm sorry, I'm sorry." Maltravers decided that firmness was needed to prevent him spiralling into virtual hysterics.

"I insist," he said. "This is obviously important."

"Well, if you're quite sure . . ." Plainly the cleric was not sure of anything. Feeling that actually hauling him inside the house would be excessive, Maltravers extended a friendly arm which caught him in an invisible scoop of hospitality.

"I am quite sure. Come in," he said briskly. "I think the study would be best," he added, having landed his frightened fish. "I'll go and fetch the Canon."

He herded the visitor into Michael's study which lay immediately off the hall, by the front door, then paused as he returned to the kitchen.

"I'm sorry," he said. "But you are . . . ?"

"Matthew Webster. The cathedral Succentor."

"Of course," said Maltravers, although there was no of course about it, and went to inform Michael.

"Off Targett, as it were," he said as he re-entered the kitchen. "One Matthew Webster to see you and I have the distinct feeling it's urgent."

"Matthew Webster?" said Michael. "What on earth does he want?"

"That I didn't discover but he's in your study."

"Didn't you tell him I was busy?"

"No. You're not, and even if you were I would have suggested that you see him. He is a very anxious young man."

Michael made some ill-defined sound of impatience, a loose alliance of a sniff and a grunt, and went out of the room.

"What's troubling Matthew now?" said Melissa with the air of a woman who has been much tried.

"It's obviously nothing trivial," replied her brother. "The man's on a knife-edge."

Melissa sighed. "He frequently is. He's very . . . earnest is Matthew. Everything is taken very seriously. He lives in a state of perpetual drama. Even the Bishop finds his sincerity trying at times."

"You're making him sound like a saint," said Maltravers. "And I've always thought they must have been a pain in the neck to live with. Who is he anyway? I don't remember meeting him before."

"He's our Succentor — the first time we've had a deputy Precentor. The Bishop appointed him after finding when he ordained him that Matthew has a particular talent for music. He's a very good organist as well and is unofficial deputy to old Martin Chamberlain, which is invaluable at the moment because Martin's been in hospital for weeks." She sighed. "But his faith can be somewhat over-fervent. Whatever he's come about it's probably only of burning importance to himself."

Further speculation was interrupted by the actual arrival of Miss Targett, a wispy lady well struck in years, with the manner of one who would quite welcome her maiden sensitivities being offended, as though she would whisper very naughty words with a thrill of excited horror. Melissa brought her into the kitchen, having explained Michael's absence, and the briefest of introductions was sufficient for her to treat three complete strangers as lifelong intimates.

"Oh, my dears," she began in excited tones as she sat down and pulled off decorative summer gloves of fine white cotton. "What a business this all is! The Latimer Mercy gone and me being the first to notice it! Well, I don't know what made me even

24

look, it's not as though I make a point of these things. After all, I must have passed it hundreds of times without even a glance but, you know, something *made* me take notice and what do you think? Gone. Vanished. Stolen. Well, I didn't know what to do. Nobody in sight and at that time of the morning who could I tell? However, I . . ."

"What time was it?" asked Maltravers, daring the torrent of words.

"Pardon? The time? Oh, it must have been . . . let me see. I was just a *little* late setting off because Sebastian — that's my little cat — had gone wandering off and I was looking for him to make sure he was safely locked up. Then on the way I met Miss Templeton — oh, Melissa, my dear, have you heard that her niece has had another little baby? That's the fourth. Who would have thought it from such a tiny thing? Well, we had quite a chat about all that, then I said I must be getting on and I went straight to the shop — of course I was still there before that wretched Morgan woman — and opened up and checked the till and everything. Then I spoke to one of the vergers . . . no, I tell a lie, there were two people who came in and bought some cards . . . *then* I spoke to the verger. What was it about? Oh, I don't recall. Then the Morgan woman arrived and, of course, insisted on checking the till again so I watched her do that (then there couldn't be any arguments) then I went for a quick walk round. I always like it in the cathedral when it's so quiet and peaceful. Now, let's see . . . I went round by the Lady Chapel because the window always looks so gorgeous with the morning sun behind it, then . . . yes, I must have walked all the way round the building before I reached the display case, so . . ." Miss Targett smiled brightly at four faces suspended in expressions of polite attention. ". . . it must have been about half past ten," she concluded. "Or so."

"Half past ten," repeated Maltravers, filled with anticipatory sympathy for the elaborate narratives Jackson would have to endure in pursuit of a statement.

"Well, yes, although now I think about it . . ." Miss Targett began again.

"No, no, that will be fine," Maltravers interjected hastily. "A

25

reasonable approximation will suffice. Obviously, there wouldn't be a great many people around at that time. The cathedral opens at what time?"

"Nine o'clock," replied Miss Targett with unaccustomed brevity.

"Nine o'clock. Then . . . no it could obviously have been taken last night and nobody noticed it until you did. Tell me . . ." Maltravers broke off as Miss Targett became suddenly excited.

"Oh!" she cried. "You're . . . you're . . . oh, I know you . . . you're . . ." She was staring with wide eyes across the table.

"Diana Porter," said Diana.

"Of *course*! Oh my dear, my apologies for not recognising you at once. I saw you on the television. Your readings from Julian of Norwich were *so* beautiful. You know I keep a copy by my bedside and read them every night, but you put so much *meaning* into them. I'm so delighted to . . ." And Miss Targett fluttered her hands eloquently, finding even her own powers of speech inadequate.

"Thank you, Miss Targett," said Diana. "It's always a great pleasure to find that one's work is so appreciated."

Miss Targett, one of the countless thousands to whom those who appear on television are thought of as some form of rare and elevated beings and whose attention is as overwhelming as that of actual Royalty, brimmed with pleasure.

"Oh, my dear," was all she could say, but the cadences of the three words and subtle touches of body language acknowledged a deep sense of her unworthiness for such thanks. Maltravers fondly imagined her subsequent retelling of the moment, embroidered with happy, if untrue, embellishments, to the awe and envy of her acquaintances.

"Of course, Miss Davy is also an actress," he put in.

"Oh, really," said Miss Targett, reluctantly pulling herself away from the magnetic charm of Diana's courtesy. "I don't think I've seen . . . ?"

"I do most of my work on stage," said Tess, rightly calculating that the locations and nature of her work were not within Miss Targett's sphere of interest.

"Oh, well, never mind, perhaps one day you will . . ." she

responded graciously and Maltravers cut short her progress down a rather dangerous conversational route by deliberately knocking over a carafe of water. The resulting minor chaos saved Miss Targett from receiving the icier edges of Tess's tongue and covered the sound of Michael closing the front door after the departing Webster.

"What did Matthew want?" asked Melissa as he returned to the kitchen.

"Oh, he's very concerned about the theft," he replied. "You know what he's like."

Melissa clearly did, but Maltravers grasped the opportunity of inquiring in order to avoid further conversational problems with Miss Targett about total theatrical nonentities who languished in the obscurity of the West End.

"Well, he's very sincere," Michael explained. "He's quite appalled that something like this should happen in the cathedral."

"But he has no responsibility, has he?"

"None at all. His job is the cathedral music. But he has a very strong sense of the dignity and holiness of the church generally."

"I would hope his fellow clergymen shared it," Maltravers observed.

"Well, of course," said Michael, who was in no mood to rise to another session of religious baiting from his brother-in-law. "But Matthew can be . . ." He sought the word.

"Excessive," said Melissa.

"Yes . . . zealous . . . over-dedicated might be better. I'm afraid this business has upset him dreadfully. I've spent the last few minutes trying to calm him down and comfort him. He said he was going to the cathedral to pray. He does that a lot."

"I thought you all did," said Maltravers mischievously. "It's part of the Contract of Employment isn't it?"

"At the moment, Augustus, I have too much on my mind to enter into another futile discussion on matters about which you know little but say a great deal," said Michael loftily. "Miss Targett, I think we should be on our way."

Miss Targett's attention had irresistibly rotated back to Diana, feeding itself with discreet glances. Blatant staring had been

27

exorcised as bad manners in a long-ago childhood. Her disappointment at being summoned from the Presence was instant and obvious, but immediately covered by polite behaviour. She was consoled by an inner hope that further meetings might occur while Diana was in Vercaster. Their departure was briefly delayed by the arrival of a reporter and photographer from the *Vercaster Times* whose cathedral contacts had tipped them off about the Latimer Mercy theft long before the official police announcement. Michael was clearly annoyed by their inopportune if enterprising appearance and Maltravers diplomatically took over, ushering them both into the study. The reporter was young and enthusiastic, the photographer, many years his senior, resigned to waiting through the entire interview before he could start work.

"I'm sorry, but I don't know who you are," the young man began with commendable frankness.

"I'm actually Canon Cowan's brother-in-law, but I know quite a lot about this. My name's Augustus Maltravers."

"Oh, the writer," said the reporter and Maltravers acknowledged his cognizance. "I'm going to write a book one day."

"Most of your tribe are," said Maltravers. "Some of my best friends in Fleet Street want to be writers; in fact most of them have been talking about it for years. Now, what do you want to know?"

The information was gathered in an eccentric mixture of scribbled longhand and shorthand outlines unknown to Pitman, although the questioning was impressively thorough. The photographer, who appeared to have mastered the art of silent, and hopefully profitable, meditation, lumbered to life when the question of a picture was raised and Maltravers despatched them to the cathedral, mendaciously assuring them that the Canon had indicated approval of their activities.

"Oh, and how old are you?" the reporter asked as they were leaving.

"I can't see that's of the slightest relevance," Maltravers told him. "However, Canon Cowan is sixty-eight and carries his years remarkably well. You may quote me on that. Goodbye."

Grinning ridiculously to himself, Maltravers went to the living-room where Diana and Tess were expressing increasing amaze-ment and dismay at the varying fortunes of their contemporaries.

"You're joking!" Tess was exclaiming as he entered the room. "He could only have landed a part like that by sleeping with somebody and I don't dare think who it was."

"This is no conversation for a cathedral city," said Maltravers. "You will corrupt the Godly. Anyway, we must go and look at the Chapter House."

The building was closed to the public for the day while a low circular wooden stage was set in its centre, surrounded by tiered rows of chairs. The work had been finished by the time they arrived and they had the place to themselves. Diana stepped onto the temporary platform and gazed all around her.

"Augustus, it's beautiful!" she exclaimed.

"Well, I tried to describe it, but it's one of those places you have to see to believe," he said. "The only thing to exceed it is probably Henry VII's chapel at Westminster which was built around the same time. More to the point, the acoustics are very good, although they probably didn't plan that."

"Can we run through part of it?" Diana asked.

"Yes. I assumed you'd want to. Let's try the opening and the end. We've got plenty of time and nobody is likely to come in because they've put signs up."

Maltravers and Diana had rehearsed the performance pre-viously in London with only Tess for an audience. She and Maltravers sat in silence for half an hour watching the final result.

"What do you think?" asked Diana as she finished.

"What I've thought for a long time," said Tess. "You won't just do this on one night in Vercaster." She turned to Maltravers. "Why don't you write things like this for me?"

"Because, my love, you are not Diana. And you know it. Come on, I'll show you the rest of the geography."

They left the Chapter House and walked down a short passage to another door which opened onto a covered corridor running at right angles. Facing them was a series of stone arches which looked onto the quadrangle of the cloisters.

"This, you will be fascinated to learn, is the slype," said Maltravers. "It's a passage linking the south transept up to the right there with the Chapter House and the cloisters. I would impress you with the derivation of the word, but I don't know it. Now we go this way." He turned to the left.

They walked down the slype and went through the left door of two facing them in the end wall. It led into a small, plain, bright room filled with afternoon sun pouring through the window which looked down to the Verta over the slope of the Abbey hill.

"You can, of course, draw the curtains in the evening and, wonder of wonders, behold, modern plumbing," said Maltravers as he pulled open the door of a built-in cupboard to reveal a washbasin and mirror. "The lighting's not marvellous, I'm afraid, but excessive making up will not be necessary. Anything else you need?"

Diana smiled and shook her head swiftly. "No, that's fine." She fluttered her hands betraying some inner excitement. "That Chapter House is magical, you know the feeling? It's going to work, Gus." She suddenly threw her arms around him like a happy child.

"Come on," he said. "I'll show you the rest of the cathedral while we're here."

He took Tess's hand as they returned down the slype towards the south transept, smiling with pleasure at Diana's joy. As they passed through the cloister arches, a man walking on the opposite side heard their voices and glanced across at them. His eyes caught sight of Diana's fair hair shining in the sunlight and he stopped and stared fixedly at her until they disappeared from sight.

Chapter 3

THE THREE FACES of the Chapter House to the south and west
flamed as the early evening sun pulled down all the colours of the
world. The grey armour of St George shone like silver amid a
mosaic of ruby, emerald and gold; the shell-pink features of the
child-saint Etheldreda glowed about eyes of periwinkle blue; the
mazarine robes of the Virgin were shot with light. The colours
were held in the windows which, pitted by centuries of weather,
no longer permitted them to flood to the inside, which received
only a pale, bright lemon haze. Over the hour and a half of
Diana's performance the light would imperceptibly fade, the
audience's eyes adjusting without notice until they were watching the climax in lavender gloom. Maltravers had counted on the
additional dramatic effect, with its changing emphasis on glass
and stone, which he had first observed some years earlier when
he and Melissa had sat in the Chapter House one evening, quietly
talking about the death of their father. Melissa had warned him
that it depended on the vagaries of the weather but he had
remained confident.

"There are no Test matches on the day so rain is highly
unlikely," he had said. "Anyway, I'm sure that you and Michael
can put in a word to the Almighty."

As the audience gathered in the cockpit of chairs, he nudged
Melissa's arm and nodded to the vivid windows.

"Thank you for your prayers," he whispered.

"Don't be irreverent. You know how Michael is," she hissed
back.

"I'm just going to check with Diana. Keep my seat."

He made his way out through the entering people and walked
down the slype, safely cut off by ushers. Subconsciously, he trod
softly as he approached the door. He opened it to see Diana

31

sitting on a straight wooden chair, very still and with her eyes closed. Shutting the door quietly, he stepped past her to the window and looked through a gap in the curtains across the gravel path and down the Cathedral Field into the golden and powder blue summer evening. After a few moments he heard Diana relax behind him and he turned and smiled at her.

"You know you could play this audience on two cylinders," he said.

"But I can't play me on two cylinders," she replied. "And you can't do anything less than beautiful in a building like that. What are they like? The audience."

"Plentiful and anticipatory. And distinguished in Vercaster. Full turn out of clergy, of course, and I just saw the Mayor and his stunningly beautiful wife arrive with . . . prepare yourself . . . Lord Verta himself. But don't worry, I'm sure he's deaf."

Maltravers was being deliberately flippant. Diana had a routine of behaviour before any performance which was not superstition and certainly not affectation. Even an audience of the least discerning would receive a little bit of Diana Porter unique to the occasion. The tension needed to prepare for that offering had to be created and controlled by touchstones of established ceremony. And one of them was a few moments' inconsequential talk just before the start.

"How do you think they're going to take it?" she asked, checking her appearance finally in the mirror.

"They will certainly not be bored," he replied. "And don't worry about the quality out there. Vercaster is a fairly cultivated place within the ambience of London. What peasantry there may be will have been put off by the price of the tickets."

"Did my fee horrify them?"

"It raised the eyebrows but I soon explained the facts of life to them. Anyway, it's an absolute sell-out so they've covered their costs and made a profit to boot. Right." He glanced at his watch. "Theatre in the round here you come. Just wait here for a moment."

Maltravers went and checked with the ushers that the audience was seated then told them to close the Chapter House door. He returned to Diana and together they walked through the slype until they reached the door through which the murmur of polite voices could be heard. He took Diana's hand and looked inquiringly at her. She nodded briefly, then he opened the door and walked along the aisle left between the seats and stepped on to the stage. The voices were mixed with hesitant applause, which he stilled by beginning to speak.

"My Lord Bishop, Dean, your Worship, Lord Verta, distinguished guests, ladies and gentlemen," he said briskly. "It is my great pleasure to present the first event in the reborn Vercaster Festival. Will you please welcome into this beautiful building, in a special one-woman performance . . . Miss Diana Porter."

As he finished speaking, his eyes turned back towards the open door through which Diana walked towards him, smiling brilliantly. The applause echoing round the walls, he took her hand as she mounted the dais, then stepped back to resume his seat. Diana, her wheat-coloured hair swirling against her high-necked loose evening dress of black raw silk, with a ruby brooch at her throat, walked in a swift circle round her stage before sitting on a tall stool set in the centre. She clasped her hands in her lap and lowered her head as the applause faded to a silence that centred on her still figure.

"Has it ever occurred to you where Woman came in God's list of priorities?" she asked in a quiet voice that still carried like a bell to the peak of the ceiling. "First there was Heaven and Earth, then Night and Day, then He divided the waters and made the land and the sea, then grass and herbs and trees yielding fruit." She ticked the items off on eloquent fingers. "Then the sun, moon and stars, great whales and cattle, then all the creepy crawlies. Then along comes Adam, but of course he's busy for a while because God wants him to give everything a name."

Her voice suddenly deepened into that of a male adult losing patience with a child. "No, Adam, you can't call that a hippopotamus, we've already got one of those. How about calling it a toad? No? You don't like that? All right, have it your way, we'll call it a giraffe. Now what about this spotted thing with the long neck? No, that's silly, it just doesn't look like a hedgehog. And

33

you can't just say that 'bird' will do for all that lot with feathers
. . . now come on and concentrate."

Diana's normal voice returned. "Heaven knows how long it
took to sort it all out. And then what? Adam has absolutely
nothing to do except wander round the Garden of Eden, keeping
his sticky little fingers off the Tree of the Knowledge of Good and
Evil, and has dominion over every living thing. And what does
God decide? He needs a helpmeet." She stared in amazement.
"What on earth for? Anyway, God decides he's going to have
one and at last we have Woman . . . the last thing God made."
Diana paused and looked thoughtful as the observation went
home. "Of course, after all that practice, He must have been
getting quite good at making things," she added reflectively.

She stepped off the stool and walked to the edge of the stage to
stand directly in front of a row of senior clergy and their families,
put her head on one side and stared straight at the Bishop's
wife.

"But of course," she added slyly, "Adam hasn't just got a
helpmeet . . . he's now got someone to blame."

The two women looked at each other for a moment, then the
Bishop's wife gave the slightest smile and nod of agreement.
Maltravers, who had been watching her reaction intently,
breathed a long and quiet sigh.

"It's working," he muttered.

"You're my clever brother," Melissa whispered back.

The cross on the circle had been revealed, not as Michael's
image of Calvary on the globe, but the biological symbol for the
female and Diana proceeded to take her audience through
well-known country, regarded from a significantly different and
telling viewpoint. She told the story of Samson and Delilah in the
way Delilah saw it ("Long hair never did suit him"), redrew Ruth
as a merry widow in the field with Boaz with an eye to the main
chance, and produced a whole panoply of Biblical women —
Salome, the Queen of Sheba, Lot's wife, Martha and Mary and
the rest — now flippant, now bitter, here cynical, there com-
passionate. It was a performance balanced on the finest of lines
and she played it to perfection.

The final scene was the most delicate of all. Crumpled and

broken with grief, she knelt in the centre of the stage and whispered the last words of Mary Magdalene to the crucified Christ, a long wail of anguish without self-pity which had nothing to do with the salvation of Mankind but everything to do with love and death. As her audience watched in tense silence, they shared with her the helpless bewilderment and agony of the extremities of human sorrow. Maltravers, who had spent weeks wrestling to capture the words she spoke, was as enthralled as anyone. At the end she left the most fleeting of pauses before lifting a face stretched with emotion and wet with tears to cry, "Why hast thou forsaken me?" in a final shout of ultimate misery that filled the entire Chapter House before she sank into helpless sobbing in the silence. As the first handclap cracked out like a pistol shot — Maltravers noticed with pleasure that it was the Bishop who made it — Diana stood, then descended into a deep curtsey as applause rolled about her. She bowed to all sections of her audience before swiftly walking off the way she had entered. The applause intensified and she returned, recovering all the time, to smile and bow again. She pulled a reluctant Maltravers on stage to share her triumph before making a final exit which no demands would reverse. People settled back in their own release from emotion; then began a ragged but orderly exit through to the Refectory for coffee. Melissa turned to her brother.

"Augustus, that was wonderful," she said. "You understand women better than any man I know. Even Michael's going to have to think about that."

"Thank you," he replied as she kissed him. "But it was the word made flesh that really did it. That was the finest performance I've ever seen her give."

"She's coming through for coffee, isn't she?" Melissa asked anxiously. "I must congratulate her."

"Of course she is, but you'll have to give her a few minutes. You go on and Tess and I will go and see how she is."

As they walked towards Diana's room, Tess squeezed Maltravers' arm but did not speak.

"I know," he said simply. "Let's go and bring her down to earth."

Diana had opened the curtains and was standing by the

35

window staring at the darkening landscape as they entered. Maltravers crossed the room and put his hands on her shoulders.

"You do my work more honour than I fear my work can bear," he said.

"Thank you," she said. "It was good, wasn't it?"

"That's one way of putting it. Miraculous would be nearer."

Diana turned and looked at Tess. "What do you think?"

"That I may as well quit now," she replied.

"You're being ridiculous and you know it." Diana laughed and held her hands out to both of them. "But I'm so glad it was special and that you two approve."

She threw her arms around Maltravers and he felt the tension flow out of her.

"Come on," he said. "Your public is waiting in the Refectory and they were a very good audience."

"Weren't they marvellous? You know what the moment was that made it start to work? That bit right at the beginning about Adam having someone to blame. I thought that woman would never react! Who was she?"

"The Bishop's wife."

Diana pulled an exaggerated face of mock horror. "I was that near to dying on a Saturday night in Vercaster?"

"I nearly went with you. I knew who she was."

The three of them made their way round the Refectory where, to Maltravers' amusement, Diana gave another finely judged if minor performance of the persona meeting her public. There were repeated congratulations, now effusive, now more tellingly brief, until they reached the group of principal guests where Maltravers introduced her to the Bishop, a small delicate man with light grey hair above a florid and cheerful face.

"Miss Porter," he said, giving the nearest gesture possible to a bow without diminishing the dignity of crook and mitre. "I find it difficult to express the pleasure you have given this evening. At my age I do not expect to have to re-examine long-held beliefs but you have given many of us food for thought. Let me introduce you."

Maltravers stepped back and collected his coffee while, looking engagingly like a proud father with his glittering daughter,

36

the Bishop ushered her round his attendant group. As he watched, Maltravers felt a touch on his sleeve and turned round to find it was Jackson.

"Hello," he said. "On or off duty?"

"On. I just thought it possible I might spot somebody or something here that might throw light on the theft."

"And did you?"

"No," Jackson smiled. "But I got to see Miss Porter so it was well worth it."

"I take it there have been no developments?"

Jackson shook his head. "Nothing at all so far, although it's early days yet. There's no known pattern it fits into that we can see. I'm just hoping we've closed all possible exit routes out of the country."

Maltravers' attention was distracted by the Bishop calling his name and he joined him and Diana. They were standing with the Mayor and Mayoress and assorted clergy.

"I understand you wrote tonight's work, Mr Maltravers," the Bishop said.

"With a little help from the Bible, Bishop."

"Well, we must congratulate you as well. Some very remarkable interpretations. Tell me, have you ever considered entering the church yourself?"

Maltravers heard Melissa, who was standing nearby, splutter into her coffee.

"No," he replied. "I think I would have difficulty with some of the teaching." To his relief, the Bishop did not pursue the point. Even though Maltravers had spent many years deliberately arguing with, trying to undermine and even mocking his brother-in-law's beliefs, the Bishop was not family. The Dean, who had just joined the group, began congratulating Diana, which gave Maltravers the opportunity to withdraw.

"Very self-controlled," Melissa murmured. "The Bishop is much too gentle a Christian for your astringency."

"He approved of what I wrote," said Maltravers.

"Yes, but you trod very softly for once. Incidentally, don't look now, but there's a man just behind you to your right who keeps staring over this way. By the door. I've been watching him for several minutes and he can't seem to keep his eyes off Diana."

"Well, she is the star attraction," said Maltravers. "You know what people are like with the famous. Remember Miss Targett."

"Yes, but it's . . . I don't know. I just don't like the way he keeps looking."

"I take it you don't recognise him."

"No. I'm sure he's nothing to do with the cathedral. I wondered if you might . . . oh, damn, he's gone."

Maltravers turned instinctively and looked towards the Refectory door which had been left open.

"What did he look like?" he asked.

Melissa shrugged. "Oh, quite ordinary. I was probably imagining things. Didn't like it though. More coffee?"

It was nearly eleven o'clock when they left the cathedral for the short walk through a velvet summer night back to Punt Yard, where they had a final drink before going to bed.

"When do you have to leave tomorrow?" Melissa asked Diana.

"Oh, sometime in the afternoon. What time are the trains? As long as I'm back in town by Monday morning."

"Fine. Michael's taking morning service at St John's tomorrow, so perhaps you three would like to take Rebecca out while I do lunch. And you are coming to the Dean's garden party in the afternoon?"

"Of course," said Diana. "He was very insistent. It doesn't matter which train I get back."

Maltravers and Tess stayed up after the rest had gone to bed and talked.

"She crossed a few frontiers tonight," Tess remarked.

"She did indeed. And just think what she's got to do. Desdemona, Juliet, Cleopatra, Ophelia. She's going to find things in there that even the blessed William didn't imagine."

Tess looked at him as he stared reflectively into the empty fireplace, still attracting the gaze even without winter coals, and knew his mind was full of rich imaginings. For nearly three years she had felt secure with him because she had learned that one part of him would always be under the witchcraft of words, written or spoken, and had recognised she must not invade that private world. And these feelings she could share; she was an actress herself and had seen her art performed at the highest level by a woman who was also her friend. They sat for a while recalling Diana Porter's greatest performance, then went to bed.

Chapter 4

PLUMP AND WELL-FED ducks paddled at the water's edge as
Tess, Diana and Rebecca dropped torn pieces of bread into an
ill-mannered splatter of beaks. A quarter of a mile away the
cathedral bells rang mathematically, their tones mixing dis-
cordantly with the electric chimes of an ice-cream vendor's
van playing a syncopated snatch of *Greensleeves* as it drew
to a halt in the car-park at the edge of the Verta's water
meadows. While Rebecca laughed at the antics of the ducks,
a kestrel hovered against crystalline blue, high across the river,
while swifts flashed low over the surface of hammered silver
water.

"The world is charged with the grandeur of God," remarked
Maltravers. "I cannot share the unhappy Gerard's beliefs, but
I'm with him there."

They had attended morning service in the cathedral among a
congregation filled with turning heads, nudges and whispers as
they took their places. Michael was still at the distant St John's
and Melissa was producing dishes concomitant with various beds
of rice.

Tess took Maltravers' arm and a now adoring Rebecca held
Diana's hand as they walked upstream to the remains of a
derelict Saxon church, abandoned when the cathedral was built.
Misshapen sections of wall still stood, including one entire arch
which must have encompassed the door. Once through it, there
were enough remains to assess the dimensions and general shape
of the original building.

"It was very tiny," said Diana.

"Well, between the Romans departing and Etheldreda
coming all over in a religious faint, Vercaster was not exactly
a metropolis," said Maltravers. "You could probably have

accommodated about eighty people in here which would have been quite adequate."

"Is it still hallowed ground?" Tess asked.

"It may be. I'm never sure how one dehallows places. Or is it unhallow? It's certainly still on cathedral land but with great lumps of the Roman wall of the city remaining, it doesn't even rate as a tourist attraction."

They sat on the grass with their backs against the remains of one wall and Diana made a daisy chain for Rebecca, placing the tiny circlet of flowers on her brown shining hair.

"One for you as well," Rebecca demanded.

"All right. Go and find some more daisies."

Maltravers watched the attractive proceedings with interest.

"This maternal instinct is something new," he said. "I've never known you take any interest in children before."

"I'm very fond of them," Diana replied, carefully poking one daisy through the split stem of another. She turned to Rebecca. "And if I ever have a little girl, I'm going to call her after you. There." She placed the completed chain of flowers on her hair. "Titania, perhaps?" Distantly they heard the cathedral clock.

"I shall forgo the obvious quote, but it's time we were getting back for lunch," said Maltravers. "Then it's the Trollopian gathering at the Dean's."

Over lunch he speculated on finding a Slope, Proudie or Septimus Harding at the event.

"You will behave," Melissa told him sharply. "You are our guest."

"Yes, big sister," he replied meekly.

"And I'm not your big sister. I'm five years younger."

"Perhaps. But you always *seemed* like one."

The Dean's house was in Cathedral Close which ran parallel with Punt Yard from opposite the Chapter House. Maltravers waited on the front doorstep for the others before they set off for the short walk and noticed a man on the opposite side of the Yard looking closely at the house. He had thinning, swept back hair and wore an open-necked check shirt. He suddenly realised Maltravers was staring back at him and walked briskly away

41

towards the main road at the opposite end of the Yard from the cathedral.

"Queer bird. I wonder who he was?" Maltravers said as Tess joined him.

"Who?"

"Chap just going round the corner. Another of the Vercaster starers."

"He's just a tourist. The place is full of them. Come on, here are the others."

They were greeted by the Dean's formidable wife, a woman, Maltravers whispered to Tess, of remarkable bosom who shepherded them straight through the house and out of the French windows into the garden, already adorned with sundry clerics either stationary or moving with slow and seemly tread. The garden was enormous — Maltravers learned later that it was nearly three quarters of an acre — with a massive, impeccable lawn between two lines of towering dark rhododendron bushes set behind flower beds. Other smaller bushes and beds dotted the grass which ran down to an assorted collection of mature trees and associated undergrowth that had been left to its natural devices and formed the last third of the garden. The whole effect was of total privacy, the similar adjacent gardens behind the terrace of homes quite invisible. Maltravers pondered its possibilities as a suitable gathering place for Vercaster nudists and amused himself by mentally stripping its present occupants of cassock, purple waistcoat or dignified gaiter but stopped abruptly when his gaze reached the Dean's wife.

As he had anticipated, the occasion was Barchester revisited, the conversations polite and muted, the acknowledgements of clerical seniority subtly observed. He and Tess spent some time talking to a very young curate and his wife who suddenly confessed a nervous craving for a cigarette but feared the wrath of the Dean's wife at a stub despoiling the pristine perfection of the grass. Maltravers sympathetically suggested a stroll to the sanctuary of the woods at the end of the garden and they made their way through the trees to the boundary fence which looked over some twenty yards of river bank to the Verta. They returned to be separated by the Dean's wife who clearly held the darkest suspicions about what they had been up to. Tess and Maltravers were firmly escorted to meet the rector of a distant parish who had apparently expressed a desire to talk to them, while the curate's wife was withered by a look that augured little prospect of her husband's advancement in the diocese. As they talked, Maltravers saw Diana, escorted by their host, circulating among the guests, each group opening up with released anticipation as she approached. Wherever she went laughter filled that part of the garden.

"Such a charming young woman," said a voice at Maltravers' elbow and he turned to face the horizontal mountains of his hostess. "We are so delighted she could attend. Are you enjoying yourselves?" There was no time to reply; having acknowledged their presence as the unavoidable price to pay for having Diana there, the Dean's wife moved formidably on.

Tea was naturally served in fine and thin china, with slender sandwiches with sliced summer fillings carried on matching plates. It was an exquisitely mannered, civilised gathering of clerical gentlefolk which Maltravers, although he might later mock it unmercifully, found thoroughly enjoyable.

"The only thing that puzzles me is, isn't this your working day?" he asked a rector who was juggling cup, saucer and plate with some dexterity. "I know the Founder made it a day of rest but don't you all have to go and preach somewhere or something?"

"Yes. Most of us have evensong and some of those who have to travel a fair distance have already left." Maltravers realised that the numbers had been slowly thinning out.

"In fact," the rector gulped his remaining tea with unseemly haste from such a container, ". . . if you will excuse me, I'd better be off."

Evensong at the cathedral was at half past six and by five past the garden was deserted again, its occupants having left no visible trace of their presence. Tess, Maltravers, Michael and Melissa were on the terrace saying goodbye.

"Thank you so much, Dean," Michael said. "It has been delightful but I really must get over to the cathedral."

"Of course," replied the Dean. "But I must say goodbye to Miss Porter. Where is she? I had to leave her a little while ago when the Bishop left and . . ." He looked at them with polite inquiry and there was an air of slight puzzlement as their glances swept over the empty garden.

"I saw her a few minutes ago," said Tess. "She was down there." She pointed towards the trees at the bottom of the garden.

"Who was she with?" asked Maltravers.

"I don't know. I think she was on her own but I didn't really notice."

"Perhaps she's in the house," said the Dean's wife briskly. "No, you stay here and I'll go and find her."

As they waited on the terrace, a bank of cloud drifted across the slow-falling sun and brightness went out of the garden. Tess took Maltravers' arm and shivered slightly.

"Chilly," she said with a small smile.

"Well, she's not in there." Returning through the French windows, the Dean's wife sounded slightly put out; one of her guests was behaving badly.

A search of the gardens by Maltravers and an increasingly impatient Michael revealed nothing and finally, with suitable apologies, they left, the Dean dismissive and understanding, his wife clearly far from pleased.

"Where the hell is she?" Maltravers demanded as they left the house.

"Perhaps she's gone back to Punt Yard," said Tess.

"Not without saying goodbye," he said firmly.

Diana was not at Punt Yard although her suitcase, ready packed for her return to London, was still in the hall. One of Melissa's friends, who had brought her own daughter round to play with Rebecca while they were out, had not seen her. They waited for a quarter of an hour before Maltravers became impatient and set off to look without having any real idea of where to go. He walked round to the cathedral but the verger on the west door assured him that Diana had not been there. Then he went back to the river and the ruined church. Diana had never been to Vercaster before and there were very few places she had seen.

"This is getting ridiculous!" he snapped when he returned to Punt Yard and found she had not turned up in his absence.

"Where's Diana?" Rebecca asked suddenly, looking up from where she was playing on the floor.

"Did Diana say bye-bye to you?" Melissa asked her.

"No," said the child simply and the three adults stared at each other.

Maltravers took a drink proffered by his sister and lit a cigarette, exhaling the smoke noisily and agitatedly through his teeth.

"Now, let's get this straight," he said. "You say you saw her, Tess, standing near the trees at . . . what? . . . sometime after six o'clock. None of us saw her after that. And you say there was nobody with her."

"I don't remember seeing anyone. But they could have been hidden by the trees."

"What was she doing?"

"Just standing there."

"Talking?"

Tess thought for a moment. "No. But if there had been someone I couldn't see, she might have been listening."

"All right," said Maltravers. "Can she have gone back to town? Her case is still here."

"She had her handbag," said Tess. "Her train ticket was in there along with her purse."

"So . . . no that's stupid. She's not said goodbye to anybody. Not even Rebecca. Where the devil is she?"

Nobody had any answers and Diana's disappearance lay about them as Rebecca was put to bed. Michael returned and they ate a cold supper at the end of which Maltravers announced he was going to ring Diana's London flat. He returned after a few minutes to say there was no reply.

"Do you think we should tell the police?" Melissa asked.

"What are they going to do? Not launch a manhunt for what appears to be no more than inexplicable bad manners."

"Her case is still here," observed Tess.

"Precisely. She could just be wandering round the town somewhere. It's totally unlike her, but I don't think the police are going to get too excited."

They spent the rest of the evening watching television in an abstracted sort of way with Maltravers making regular calls to Diana's flat and various friends without success. Finally, at nearly midnight, he did call the police.

The duty sergeant listened to everything he had to say, then asked a series of questions which took them over the same ground again.

"Have you tried all her friends?" he asked.

"Well, that's a lot of people and I don't know them all. I've tried about a dozen so far."

"I think that's the best thing to do at the moment, sir," said the sergeant. "Just a minute. You say she came up by train. Have you checked at the station?"

"No, I hadn't thought of that."

"Well, we can do that, sir. Can you tell me what the young lady was wearing?"

"Oh, God, I don't know. Hang on." Maltravers called Tess to the phone who supplied the details then handed the receiver back to him.

"Right, sir, you keep trying her friends and I'll let you know if there's any news from the station. If you can give me your number." Maltravers read it from the dial. "All right. Thank you. I don't imagine there's anything to worry about but I'll pass this on. You just make what inquiries you can for the time being."

As he rang off, Maltravers realised it was no time of night to be ringing people to see if they knew where Diana was, but decided to try anyway. He managed three calls, met with varying degrees of politeness, before the sergeant came back to him to say there had been no sign of Diana at the station.

"I'm sure the young lady will turn up quite safe, sir, but let us know first thing in the morning if there's no news. I'm sure there's nothing to worry about. Goodnight, sir."

After reluctantly going to bed, Maltravers lay in the darkness

46

thinking. His bedroom door opened quietly and Tess came in.

"Move over," she said, crossing to the bed. "Damn the proprieties, I'm not leaving you on your own tonight." She settled down and put her arm around him. "She'll turn up. It will be all right in the morning."

But it wasn't. Maltravers rang Diana's flat again first thing but there was still no reply. He tried a few other calls without success, then rang the police again. It was the same sergeant on duty.

"Nothing at all, sir? Just a moment, I'm putting you through to the duty Inspector. She knows the background."

As various clicks sounded down the line into Maltravers' ear, Diana's disappearance ceased to be a minor problem and became a police matter, sweeping Maltravers and the others along on the rising tide of an official investigation. The Inspector, female, crisp and businesslike, took what little new information there was then told Maltravers to remain at the house until an officer arrived; in fact it was Jackson again. Maltravers, who had imagined that the police would take little interest in an adult who had disappeared for less than twenty-four hours, was at first impressed, then alarmed, by the level of their activity.

"A few years ago it might have been different," Jackson told him. "Now we press the panic buttons much sooner."

He began close questioning Maltravers and Tess as the people who knew Diana best. Had she seemed depressed? Unusually excited? Was she worrying about anything? Had she ever talked about taking her life? Maltravers stared at him.

"Don't be stupid," he snapped.

"It's not stupid. It's an obvious line of inquiry. Can you give me her exact address in London please."

"What for?"

"We'll want to talk to the neighbours. And we'll want to get in there."

"What the hell do you expect to find?"

"We expect nothing. But we might find Miss Porter."

"She's not there. I've told you how many times I've rung."

"Perhaps she can't answer the phone," Jackson said levelly.

"Why not, for Christ's sake?"

Jackson paused, sighed and shook his head.

"I'm sorry, but I'm going to have to spell this out," he said. "Miss Porter is a well-known person, but in these circumstances we'd do the same whoever it was. She has disappeared without explanation and we have to look at all the possibilities. You say she didn't appear suicidal but some people don't give any indication. I don't want to add alarm or distress to the situation because I appreciate that you are increasingly worried, but the simple fact is that she may be in her flat and unable to answer the phone because she has taken her own life. I don't expect you to accept the possibility but it is one that the police have got to consider."

"You can't just break into her flat," Maltravers objected.

"We can with a warrant. And, believe me, in these circumstances we'll get one."

Maltravers slumped back in his chair, defeated by police procedures and Jackson's reasonableness. He remembered Diana's elation after her performance, her laughter at the garden party, her total air of being relaxed and happy. But that was meaningless to the police; people who vanished followed certain statistical patterns of behaviour offering a finite series of options. He realised that all he could do was to co-operate.

"I've just remembered something," he said. "Diana had an appointment in London this morning. I don't know where but her agent will. Shall I ring him?"

Jackson nodded with an air of excessive patience.

"If you would," he said.

Joe Goldman metaphorically leapt at Maltravers down the phone.

"Gus!" he shouted. "Where the hell's Diana?"

"You've not heard from her?"

"No! We're due at the BBC in ten minutes. I've tried her flat but she doesn't answer. Vanished? What do you mean vanished? Suddenly she's a conjuring act? Jokes I don't need, Gus."

"It's no joke. We've got the police up here."

"The fuzz? Diana Porter disappears at a vicarage garden party and now the police are in on it?" His voice began to rise through uniquely Jewish octaves. "It's big break country at the BBC,

Gus! Today's visit cost me three lunches. Find the bloody stupid cow!"

Maltravers, his own emotions rising, did all he could to calm him down but without effect.

"You find her and I want to be the second person to know," yelled Joe. "I'll put the Beeb off with some story but get her here!" The phone slammed down at the other end.

When Maltravers returned to Jackson another policeman had arrived.

"You said that was Miss Porter's case in the hall? This officer will need a piece of her clothing from it for the dogs."

"Dogs? What dogs?"

"They're at the Dean's at the moment and are starting a search of the garden, although with the numbers of people there I'm not too optimistic." Jackson noticed the look of amazement on Maltravers' face. "There's a team of frogmen on their way to the Verta as well," he added. "Miss Davy, would you be so kind as to open Miss Porter's case for this officer and find something suitable?

"The only other thing at the moment," he continued, "is are you aware of any threats that may have been made against Miss Porter?" Maltravers shook his head. "All right, we'll see if there's anything in her flat or if her neighbours know anything. We'll need full statements from you and everybody else who was at the garden party. Try to remember everything, who she talked to, anything she said. And in your case, anything from the time she arrived in Vercaster up to the time she disappeared. However insignificant, it might help. You don't happen to have a picture of her do you?"

"Not here. Why?"

"Well, we're obviously going to have to release this to the Press, although they probably have pictures on file anyway."

"Look, aren't you going a bit overboard on this?" asked Maltravers.

"It's like your Latimer Mercy," said Jackson. "We're going to warn all ports to watch out for her, we're going to inform other police forces. What do you want us to do? Shrug our shoulders and hope she'll turn up and then discover we've made some dreadful error of judgement? We get a lot of stick for doing that. If it turns out that we've over-reacted there's nothing lost. But there's going to be a lot of egg on our faces if it turns out we failed to take the proper steps."

The rest of the morning was resonant with the increasing crescendo of the proper steps: an outraged Dean's wife as her garden was invaded by large boots and trotting paws, balanced by a concerned and sympathetic Dean; curious sightseers watching the frogmen ruffling the slow waters of the Verta; the relentless ringing of the telephone; Joe Goldman increasingly agitated and unreasonable; Miss Targett alarmed and inquisitive; the Bishop shocked; reporters who had somehow traced Maltravers; never news of Diana.

To provide their official statements, Maltravers and the others searched their memories for details of events they had hardly noticed, while the same process was going on throughout the diocese with all the rest of the Dean's guests. By mid-afternoon, frustrated by his own inertia in the midst of all the activity, his initial mystification about Diana's disappearance climbing a rising scale of worry, Maltravers was pacing the house and chain smoking.

"What about loss of memory?" Tess said suddenly. "It happens."

"Now there's something we haven't tried," he said. "She could be anywhere. Checked in under a false name in a Frinton guest house. Caught a plane to Outer Mongolia. Entered a bloody nunnery."

"I'm trying to help!" Tess snapped.

"What sort of goddamned help is loss of memory?"

"Stop it, the pair of you!" Melissa interrupted. "I know Diana was your friend and you're both worried, but she was also a guest in our home and, even though we hardly knew her, we happened to like her very much. This is bad enough for everyone without you two starting a slanging match." She glared at them as they both apologised. "That's better. Now, it may not seem very important to you at the moment, but the festival is still going on and it's the first of the Mystery Plays tonight. You both said you'd come and you may as well let it take your minds off all this for a while and let the police get on with their job. Now just find something to do for a couple of hours."

Tess went to wash her hair and have a bath while Maltravers looked in Michael's study for a book to occupy his mind. Passing over the shelves of religious and ecclesiastical volumes, he picked up a copy of *Brewer's Phrase and Fable* and flicked idly through until he spotted a section on misprinted Bibles. The Latimer Mercy theft had been completely driven from his mind but, as he read the list of variously erroneous editions, he turned over the possibility of a connection between the theft and Diana's disappearance but could see none. His mind was still considering it as he told Melissa he was going for a stroll round the cathedral.

He was pounced on by Miss Targett, who leapt out from behind the tourists' shop stall as he entered the south transept, the phrases of concern, heightened by her brief meeting with Diana, rushing at him like a torrent. As he made suitable responses in what fleeting intervals she afforded him, he glanced round for a means of escape and suddenly saw the Succentor.

"Mr Webster!" he called in desperation and relief. "If you have a moment? If you'll forgive me Miss Targett, I really must . . ." and he made a swift retreat to where Webster was looking towards him in a puzzled manner.

"Sorry about that," he said as he reached him. "You were a passing means of salvation from Miss Targett."

Webster smiled understandingly. "She can be a little trying," he said. "Let's go this way." They walked towards the Lady Chapel end of the cathedral, out of sight of Miss Targett.

"I've just been giving a statement to the police about Miss Porter," Webster continued. "I remember talking to her at the garden party but I don't think I was able to give them any useful information. This must be dreadfully worrying for you all. What with this and the Latimer Mercy business I don't think there have ever been so many policemen about the cathedral."

"I'm afraid this latest business is causing a great deal of upset all over the place," Maltravers replied. Then, as the reason for his going to the cathedral was to try and stop dwelling on the subject of Diana, he turned the conversation back to the Latimer Mercy.

"I've just been reading about misprinted Bibles and I didn't realise there were so many," he said. "I knew about the Wicked Bible which left 'not' out of the seventh Commandment, giving divine approval to adultery, but I've never heard of the Wife Hater Bible of 1810 which quoted . . . Luke was it? . . . as 'If any man come to me and hate not his father and his mother, yea and his wife also' instead of 'life'; or the one which said 'sin on more' instead of 'sin no more'. Actually the one I liked best was the Printers Bible which had David complaining 'Printers have persecuted me without cause' instead of 'Princes'. I thought it would go rather well on the desk of the Editor of the *Guardian*."

Webster smiled thinly. "Yes, I expect so, although the Bible is the word of God and personally I feel that misprinted editions are regrettable." Maltravers, remembering his reputation for sincerity, decided that further conversation on the topic would be impolite. He found clerics who could not laugh at their faith difficult.

Their conversation drifted into less contentious areas concerning the festival until they reached the north transept where Webster said he was going to see the Bishop. Maltravers continued his walk round the cathedral, pausing to read the excessive sentiments carved in marble for the ancient dead, reflecting on the singular and apparently unsullied virtues of past generations. He continued all the way round the building, passing the south transept hastily to avoid another confrontation with Miss Targett and finally sat for a while in the Lady Chapel, staring impassively at the great window of Christ enthroned that filled most of the end wall, letting the still quiet calm him. Distantly, he heard the clock in Talbot's Tower strike six and decided it was time to go back. In order to avoid the still lurking Miss Targett, he was going to leave through the north transept and walk round the outside of the cathedral but as he stood up he noticed a small door in the south wall of the Lady Chapel which, he reasoned, must be almost directly opposite Michael and Melissa's front door and would serve his purpose if it was not locked. It wasn't and did indeed stand in the relationship he had assumed, although his view of the Punt Yard house was impaired by a

52

police car parked on the double yellow lines outside. When he went inside Jackson was waiting for his return.

"Officially, I'm not here," he said. "But I thought I'd call on my way home and bring you up to date. Miss Porter is not in her flat and there's nothing we can find there that helps. We've spoken to most of the people who were at the garden party but nothing significant has emerged and the only relative we've been able to trace — her brother in Bristol — hasn't seen her for several months. I think you know her parents are dead?" Maltravers nodded.

"So she's just vanished without trace?" he said.

"Apparently. And more importantly without a reason." Jackson paused and bit his lower lip. "Look, I don't want to add to your worries but the longer it goes on like this the more serious it becomes. She's well known and she had a business appointment she would obviously keep. Twenty-four hours without anything at all is a long time in these circumstances."

"We've been thinking about loss of memory," said Maltravers. "She's never suffered from it as far as I know but it is possible."

"We know it happens but it doesn't make people invisible," Jackson commented. "Her passport's still in her flat so we can assume she's not gone abroad. Anyway, if it's any comfort, you can rest assured we're doing everything we can. The *Standard*'s carried a story with a picture in the late editions this evening and television will probably have it tonight. Tomorrow's national papers should as well, they've certainly been asking enough questions. I gather news is a bit slow at the moment, which is to our advantage."

"Thanks for calling," said Maltravers.

Jackson stood up to leave. "I never actually met Miss Porter but I saw her performance in the Chapter House and was very moved by it. I can't make promises but I'll try to keep you informed on a slightly less official basis than usual. All right?"

They shook hands and Maltravers saw him out as Tess came downstairs. They went through to join Michael and Melissa in the kitchen. Maltravers told them Jackson's news — or lack of it

— then Michael turned on the radio just as the item they were interested in was finishing.

". . . where she had been taking part in the Vercaster Festival." The announcer paused momentarily then continued, "At the London Divorce Court today a man was jailed for contempt after firing a catapult at a judge. Unemployed company director Stanley Thackery from South London said he was protesting at the amount of alimony Mr Justice Hereward had ordered he should pay to his estranged wife. The judge, who was not seriously injured, told him . . ." Maltravers turned the set off.

"Slow news day indeed," he remarked. "Anyway, we didn't miss anything we don't already know. Let's see if your Mystery Plays can take our minds off our own mystery."

Performed in the Great Hall of Vercaster's Edward VI Grammar School, a stubborn survivor in an age of more egalitarian education, the plays did entertain and occupy them. The evening was taken up with the first three plays of the cycle, the Fall of Lucifer, the Creation and the story of Adam and Eve, and Noah's Flood. The Vercaster Players destroyed all Maltravers' dark misgivings about the horrors of amateur theatre, showing themselves well rehearsed, imaginatively directed, capable of ingenious effects and entertainingly inventive. They treated the works of the monk Stephen of Vercaster with intelligent adaptation, abandoning antique and incomprehensible references for modern interpretations in modifications by the school's senior English master. They also tellingly extended the role of the Devil, introducing him throughout every play as a counterpoint to God, now evil, now mischievous, terrifying or amusing. He fell from grace with maniacal and sinister laughter, watched the creation of Adam and Eve with mouthwatering anticipation of the possibilities of corruptible innocence and caused total and hilarious havoc during the building of the ark and the loading of the animals. As the wives of Shem, Ham and Japheth tried to shepherd the children dressed as all the beasts of the world into some sort of order, the Devil constantly moved among them — he explained in an aside to the audience that he was invisible — shouting contradictory instructions until there was complete chaos. As offstage thunder rolled and Noah and his family bewailed the violence of the storm, he calmly stood to one side of the stage sheltering under a red umbrella and when the little girl dressed as the dove made her exit after delivering the olive leaf he maliciously tripped her up.

After God had bestowed his blessing upon Noah and promised mankind no further elemental wrath, the Devil watched them depart rejoicing. Then, alone on the stage, he turned to the audience to deliver his sinister valediction:

> "The end is come of storm and rain
> But Lucifer will here remain.
> About this world I here will stay
> Until the dreadful judgement day."

His eyes glittered malevolently with fiendish relish of what was to come. Then a burst of crimson smoke enveloped him and the stage plunged into darkness.

Melissa took Maltravers and Tess backstage to meet the cast and Maltravers sought out the Devil, now emerging from costume and make-up as Jeremy Knowles, a hatchet faced local solicitor whose natural expression was inescapably evil.

"You should have gone into the profession," Maltravers told him.

"You're very kind," he replied. "But I think the Vercaster Players and the local magistrates' court are as far as I want to go."

"I assume we'll be seeing more of you in the rest of the cycle?"

"Oh, yes. In Trevor's adaptation I'm hardly ever off the stage. We've taken a lot of liberties, but I think they'll work. Incidentally," he added, "I saw Miss Porter on Saturday night. Is there any news of her?"

However much he tried to put it to the back of his mind, Maltravers thought, Diana's disappearance sounded like a constant keynote. He explained briefly then returned to Tess who had been identified as an actress and was signing autographs for some of the children in the play.

"Are you an actor?" demanded a freckled redheaded boy.

"No. I'm a writer."

"Oh," said the child and managed to combine disinterest,

dismissiveness and contempt in the single syllable as he turned away. Writing, as Maltravers very well knew, was not a glamorous calling. But he felt slightly deflated by the incident. What had been a strangeness the previous afternoon had grown like an emotional cancer into a concern, a worry and now a creeping fear.

Waiting for Tess to finish, he crossed to a window and looked out over that part of Vercaster which lay below the hill on which the schóol stood. Over to the right, on its own higher hill, Talbot's Tower rose against a sky washed in blue-black ink, faintly glowing with street lights. His eyes passed casually over the irregular mosaic of slate and tiled roofs broken by glimpses of road or open space. Below one rooftop lay a cheaply furnished bedroom with slime green paint and cheap wallpaper aged to the colour of an old dishcloth in which, the previous night, Arthur Powell had slept, his precious picture of Diana Porter on the stained and cracked varnish of the table by the bed. Maltravers' gaze passed idly over it and on to the edges of the city where he could see the moving lights of distant motorway traffic.

"Goodnight!" a voice called behind him.

Maltravers turned and saw Jeremy Knowles, his face slashed by a smile that unnervingly made him look more wicked, looking towards him.

"See you again," he added, then swiftly turned and was gone.

Chapter 5

DETECTIVE CHIEF SUPERINTENDENT William Madden's head appeared to be constructed only of skull and skin without any living humanity of flesh; his hair was the colour and texture of an old tennis ball left out in all weathers. He rarely smiled, laughed only with bitterness and was so totally a professional policeman that his very plain clothes seemed as much a uniform as the one he had ceased to wear.

On Tuesday morning he sat at his desk reading the summary of the investigation into Diana's disappearance while David Jackson stood, stiff and uneasy, before him. Madden's reputation extended beyond his own force and into national police legend — ruthless, methodical, unsympathetic and very good — and Jackson had arrived at Vercaster apprehensively anticipating their first encounter. Madden, his body still, as if carved in granite, read swiftly and silently, then put the papers down and reached to adjust the position of a file tray that was fractionally out of line with the edge of his desk. Jackson waited patiently while he thought.

"Absolutely nothing? Anywhere?" he demanded.

"No, sir. We're still waiting for final reports from two of the South coast ports in case she took out a temporary passport but it doesn't seem likely."

Madden squeezed the end of his nose hard between thumb and forefinger and breathed in and out deeply; it was his only observed physical peculiarity.

"Right," he said. "Either someone's hiding her — possibly without realising it if she's in some remote hotel or something — or she's dead."

Jackson felt he was making conclusions too soon but knew better than to argue. Madden worked on the principle that co-ordinated police procedures were infallible because he was convinced that he was infallible and he expected all other police officers to be the same. He also had an impressive track record of being right.

"The problem is that we're dealing with the acting profession," Madden went on. "Emotional. Irresponsible. Artistic." He had standard definitions for nearly all classes of society, each one rarely using more than three pejorative adjectives; somehow he imagined that all life was as orderly as his desk.

"This man Maltravers. He was the one who brought her to Vercaster and was among the last to see her." He looked sharply at Jackson. "Thoughts?" he demanded, revealing that he had already thought the matter through, reached his own conclusions — which by definition must be right — and wanted to see if his subordinate could follow the same process.

"I take your point, sir, that he knows Miss Porter very well," Jackson began. Madden's logic was obvious and rooted in established patterns. If Diana Porter had been murdered it was statistically likely that the murderer was someone who knew her. Add to that the link with her presence in Vercaster, discount the possibility that unusual and therefore non-statistical forces were involved, and you ended up with Augustus Maltravers. Having reached that point, the next step was simple. Question Maltravers with increasing intensity until he gave himself away or cracked under pressure and confessed.

"But I can't see him as a potential murderer," Jackson went on, adding incautiously, "always assuming that Miss Porter has in fact been murdered." The possibility of Diana being murdered was attractive to Madden. The alternative of her hiding out with unpredictable friends meant time-consuming and irritating police inquiries; a simple murder according to oft-repeated and established patterns of human behaviour was infinitely preferable, statistically more likely and greatly more convenient.

Jackson decided it would help their future working relationship if he made his feelings clear on the matter.

"In fact, to be quite blunt, I think that the possibility of Mr

Maltravers killing Miss Porter is total crap," he said. "Sir," he added.

Madden's face rose like that of a very old turtle and stared at him like a basilisk. Jackson drew in his breath quietly and resisted the temptation to add anything that would seem to qualify and, by implication, apologise for his statement.

"Indeed?" Madden said the word quietly but with a whiplash of rising inflection, then stretched Jackson's nerve with a resonant interval of several seconds' silence which he stubbornly refused to break. Madden lowered his gaze back to the papers on his desk.

"Very well," he said. "Keep me informed on any developments." He handed back the summary impassively.

"Thank you, sir," said Jackson and left Madden's office. "That," he muttered to himself as he walked down the corridor outside, "was a damned close-run thing."

Maltravers was reading to Rebecca in the living room at Punt Yard when the telephone extension from Michael's study rang at his elbow. It was Joe Goldman.

"Gus, has she turned up?" he demanded. "She's got to be found."

"Joe, everything possible is being done. As soon as . . ."

"Do you know who called me?" Goldman interrupted excitedly. "Clive Zabinski. Yes, Zabinski, the Hollywood superbrat. He's in London, someone shows him a video of *Success City* and he wants to talk to Diana. Of course I tell him to ignore everything in the papers. It's all a misunderstanding I tell him. Of course we'll be at the Dorchester tomorrow, Mr Zabinski. Gus, when Zabinski calls you don't say the actress he wants for a new movie can't be found! *Nobody* says that to Zabinski!"

"Joe, calm down will you? We're all worried sick up here."

"*You're* worried? I'll do you a favour — I'll worry for everybody. You just find her and get her back to London by tomorrow!" The line went abruptly dead.

"Where's Diana?" asked Rebecca, still sitting on her uncle's knee. He ruffled her hair.

"I think Diana's playing a game of hide-and-seek," he said. "She's playing a joke on us."

"But I heard Mummy crying this morning," objected the child. "Not laughing."

"Look, the Wild Things are having a Wild Rumpus," said Maltravers picking up the book again. "They're not frightening at all, are they?"

"I wasn't frightened of them," Rebecca said simply. Maltravers finished the book and glanced at his watch.

"Come on," he said. "There are some appalling computer cartoons on television." Rebecca scrambled down, crossed the room and turned on the set and Maltravers went into the kitchen where Melissa was at the table peeling mushrooms.

"What's all this crying about?" he asked. "Rebecca heard you."

"Oh, you know me. The bad thoughts just got too much."

"Come on, she's just mysteriously vanished. It's all this police activity that makes it seem worse. And this morning's papers didn't help."

Faced with the standard problem of having to fill space with little sensational material, Fleet Street had practised its customary excesses, with each paper trying to outdo its rivals in imaginative headlines, eye-catching design and impact vocabulary. Diana's irrelevant nude appearance featured prominently in all the stories and her disappearance was variously a mystery, a riddle or a fear. The police in turn were baffled, concerned or involved in a search of international proportions. Maltravers usually observed such antics of newspapers obeying Frayn's Law — that journalists write for other journalists — with detached amusement, but his personal involvement on this occasion made him acutely aware of the distress such insensitive behaviour could cause.

"I know I'm being silly," said Melissa. "I'm just trying to keep busy and not think about it. What are you doing today? I'm taking Rebecca to some friends for lunch and we'll probably be there most of the afternoon. Can you amuse yourselves? Don't forget it's the cathedral concert this evening."

"We'll find something to do," he said. "We'll have lunch out and be back later."

Maltravers and Tess spent the rest of the morning buying presents for Rebecca and their hosts, then went to a pub called the Saracen's Head where a Crusader's lunch was the alternative title of the standard ploughman's. They were discussing the previous night's Mystery Plays when Jeremy Knowles approached their table bearing food and drink and asked if he might join them.

"Talk of the Devil," said Maltravers as he shuffled along the dark oak settle to make room for him.

"It's odd I should run into you," said Knowles as he sat down and arranged his lunch on the table. "Canon Cowan was telling me last night about the theft of the Latimer Mercy and this morning I had a very strange letter in the post. Here, have a look."

He produced a pale blue envelope, addressed to him at his office, which had been posted in Vercaster the previous day. It was marked "Strictly Personal" and was typed, unsigned and without any address shown at the top. While Knowles began his lunch, Maltravers began to read, passing each sheet to Tess as he finished it.

"For reasons that will become obvious," he read, "this letter has to be anonymous. It concerns the theft of the Latimer Mercy Bible from the cathedral which I read about in this morning's *Times*. The police seem to think it may have been taken abroad, but I suspect it is much nearer home. For personal reasons which I cannot go into, I do not want to approach the police directly as any information I give might be traced back to me. Of course, they will take no notice of an anonymous letter, but if you, as a local solicitor, were to approach them it would be a different matter.

"I would suggest that the Bible was stolen by (or at least for) Councillor Ernest Hibbert who, as you probably know, is a great collector of antique books. Most of them are on display in the library at his home but I happen to know that the corner cupboard in that library, which he always keeps locked, also contains a number of books which he never shows to anybody. It

61

does not matter how I discovered this but you can take my word that it is true. I would most urgently suggest that the police search that cupboard. If Councillor Hibbert objects to such a search, it will indicate his guilt.

"I have been a worshipper at Vercaster Cathedral all my life and am outraged and disgusted at this theft, particularly if, as I strongly suspect, it has been carried out by a man who considers himself a paragon of virtue in our community.

"I apologise for involving you in this matter but I have indicated my reasons above. My only connection with you is that some years ago you acted in a legal matter for me and I was impressed by your efficiency, courtesy and integrity. I regret that I now have to be discourteous and not add my name to this letter, but I am sure you will readily appreciate the position I am in."

"Any idea who it's from?" asked Maltravers as he finished reading.

"Not in the least," said Knowles through a mouthful of lasagne. "I've been in practice here for more than fifteen years so it could be any one of hundreds of people."

"Who's Ernest Hibbert?" asked Tess.

"Ernie Hibbert?" Knowles wiped the remains of the sauce off his lips. "Of course, you're not from Vercaster. The Hibberts are arguably the leading family in this city. Made their money in greengrocery, with property as a very profitable sideline."

"I bought some avocados from them the other day," Maltravers recalled. "They have a shop in the High Street."

"They've got about a dozen shops all over the county," said Knowles. "Plus owning several old Victorian houses which have been converted into very expensive flats. Ernie Hibbert is possibly the richest man in Vercaster. He was mayor a few years ago and his father and grandfather held the office before him." He indicated the letter. "If what that says is true, it's going to be a massive local scandal. Another drink?"

While Knowles was at the crowded bar, Maltravers read the letter again. It resurrected the nagging thought that the Latimer Mercy theft and Diana's disappearance might be connected but he shook his head as the idea disintegrated the more he considered it.

"What are you going to do?" he asked as Knowles returned.

"I'm not quite sure," he said, resuming his seat. "Those are serious allegations about a serious crime but, frankly, it's dynamite in Vercaster. *If* the police obtain a search warrant on the strength of that letter and the Latimer Mercy *isn't* in Hibbert's secret cupboard heads will roll all over the place. It won't do my practice any good either if it's traced back to me in any way. Perhaps you could let Canon Cowan see it."

"Do you know David Jackson?" Maltravers asked. "He's a fairly new sergeant here."

"Name rings a bell, but I haven't met him."

"Let me show it to him. If you want, I won't say it came from you, which will keep you out of it."

Knowles shrugged. "As long as you tell Canon Cowan as well. Personally, I'll be happy to be rid of it."

Their conversation moved back to the Mystery Plays and other aspects of the festival until Knowles had to return to his office.

"There's something bothering you," Tess said after he had gone.

"I haven't the remotest logical argument, but I still keep wondering if there's some sort of connection between the Latimer Mercy and Diana. Both happened at the weekend, both connected with the cathedral. But that's all. Anyway, I'll try and contact Jackson. Wait here a minute."

Maltravers rang the police station from the pub's public telephone and was put through to Jackson who listened to the news about the letter.

"Can you bring it over?" he asked. "I'd like to have a look at it."

While he was waiting for them to arrive, Jackson checked on what progress had been made in the Latimer Mercy inquiry but found that nothing had materialised. At the same time the two South coast reports he had been waiting for came in; there was no record of Diana Porter or anyone like her having been through those ports. When Maltravers and Tess arrived, he took them into an interview room and read the letter for himself.

"Where's the envelope?" he asked.

"If you don't mind, I'd rather hang onto that. The person it was sent to would rather his name were kept out of it."

Jackson sighed. "For an intelligent man, you can be remarkably stupid at times, Mr Maltravers. We're not playing games, this is a serious matter. Come on." He held out his hand, adding as Maltravers hesitated, "We can be discreet." Maltravers handed over the envelope.

"Thank you. We'll have a chat with Mr Knowles and for the time being we'll check this for fingerprints to see if anything emerges. If this is true, it gives a motive for the theft."

"I understand that Councillor Hibbert may be very heavy going," said Maltravers.

"Leave us to worry about that. Incidentally, I'm afraid there's still no news on the more important matter of Miss Porter. Obviously you've heard nothing?" They shook their heads. "All right. Thank you for bringing this in. Let me show you out.

"I shall probably see you tonight," he added as they reached the police station entrance. "I assume you'll be at the cathedral concert."

"You'll be there as well?" said Maltravers. "Duty or pleasure?"

"Pleasure. The programme looks very good. Of course, it all depends on nothing dramatic happening but I certainly hope to make it."

Goldman phoned just before they set off that evening, his agitation giving way to fatalistic resignation.

"So she blows it," he said. "Zabinski finds somebody else and her career nosedives. You know the rules, Gus. Breaks like this only happen once."

"That's the last thing on my mind at the moment. I just want Diana found."

As the four of them walked round the outside of the Chapter House on their way to the West Door entrance of the cathedral, they met the Dean, his wife and Webster walking up from Cathedral Close. The Succentor was carrying a green leather music case.

"Of course, you're playing the organ tonight," said Melissa. "I would have thought you knew it all by heart by now, Matthew."

"Just about," he said. "But I'm not so good that I can rely completely on memory."

After they had entered the cathedral, Webster went off to the organ and the rest made their way to their reserved seats. Maltravers spotted Jackson arrive and beckoned him to a spare seat next to them and, as they waited, listening to Webster's playing, he pointed out various members of the audience.

"That's the Bishop and his wife with one of the other residentiary canons. Forgotten his name but he shares the duties with my brother-in-law. Oh, and there's the Dean. Do you know him?"

"Yes. In fact I took his statement about the garden party. And his wife's." Jackson looked rueful.

"The Vercaster galleon," Maltravers grinned. "I'm afraid I don't know most of the lesser clergy, but I recognise them from the party. Oh, and there's Knowles, the solicitor who received the letter about Hibbert. Have you spoken to him yet?"

Jackson looked across the aisle to where Maltravers was indicating Knowles, engrossed in his programme.

"I don't know. I'm not handling that." Jackson regarded Knowles with interest. "That's not a face I'd relish confronting across a courtroom," he added.

"It's a face that only a mother could love, isn't it," Maltravers replied. "But he's perfectly amiable when you meet him. I'll introduce you later if we get the chance."

After a few moments Jackson stood up and gazed around, then resumed his seat.

"Where's the organ?" he asked.

"You must have seen it. It's against the south wall near where they kept the Latimer Mercy."

"That's what I thought but they're obviously going to have the choir and soloists in front of the choir screen and I can't see how the organist can see the conductor."

"Ah, modern technology," explained Maltravers. "Look at the right hand end of the top of the choir screen. See it? It's a closed circuit television camera. When the choir is in its traditional place behind the screen, the organist can see the choirmaster through a mirror, but when they're on this side they use the camera. All highly ingenious."

The lights in the nave were dimmed as the four guest professional soloists — soprano, alto, tenor and bass — took their places in front of the assembled choir and the conductor raised his baton towards the camera. The organ paused, then crashed in again on the conductor's beat and all the voices burst into "Zadok the Priest" from *Judas Maccabeus* and the concert was under magnificent way. The programme, which ran without any interval, combined expressions of religious belief in superlative music, using the individuals, choir and occasionally the congregation, who were all in the nave. The transepts and back of the cathedral were closed for the evening. The moment that caught Maltravers' delight was the soloists' unaccompanied singing of "God so Loved the World" from Stainer's *Crucifixion*, the four voices woven in perfect harmony; as they finished the organ returned with the opening bars of "Praise, my soul, the King of Heaven" in which everybody joined. Finally, choir and soloists sang the "Hallelujah Chorus" in a great shout of triumph and adoration that soared through arcade, triforium and clerestory, filling the entire building with exultant sound, the repeated words interlocking in a passion of glorification. The applause rose as they finished and the conductor beckoned through the camera for Webster to join the singers in acknowledging it.

"Who said the Devil has all the best tunes?" Maltravers remarked to Jackson.

Melissa leaned across him and invited Jackson for coffee just as Maltravers noticed Jeremy Knowles leaving. Jackson stayed with them and they were among the last to leave the cathedral, accompanied again by the Dean, his wife and Webster, who all declined a similar invitation. The two groups parted by the Chapter House and, as they entered Punt Yard, Maltravers, uplifted by the music and slightly light-headed after gins in the evening following wine at lunchtime, began to sing.

"And He shall reign for ever and e-ever! And He shall reign for ever and e-ever!" His voice echoed about the high walls of the silent yard.

"Be quiet!" snapped Michael, who disliked any excess.

"God save the King!" Maltravers blithely ignored him. "God save the King! Hallelujah! Hallelujah! Hallelujah!" He stepped in front of them and onto the doorstep.

"Augustus, shut up!" laughed Melissa.

Maltravers raised his voice in one more "Hallelujah!", then made a ridiculous bow. Michael looked irritated but the others joined Melissa's laughter as he produced a key from his pocket and made an extravagant gesture of welcome.

"Allow me!" he cried and turned dramatically towards the door, with the brass key glinting in his hand. Then his body suddenly froze.

"Jesus Christ!"

The shocked and horrified tone was more shattering than the blasphemy. The rest of them instinctively followed his transfixed stare to the front door, which stood in deep shadow, until they could make out what he had seen.

There were a few seconds of silence then Melissa screamed a terrible scream. Over the lock was nailed a severed human hand. Tess retched.

Chapter 6

"STAND STILL!" JACKSON'S shout had an imperative edge as Maltravers instinctively moved back in horror towards the door. He stopped and then Melissa screamed again.

"Rebecca!" She leapt forward but Jackson grabbed her fiercely by the arm.

"It's all right Mrs Cowan. It's not a child's hand." She struggled frantically but he dragged her back. "Canon Cowan. Would you help here, please?" Michael, his face stunned, obeyed automatically and put his arm round his sobbing wife.

"That door must not be touched," said Jackson. "Is there another way into the house?"

"There's the garden gate. We've just walked past it," said Michael. "We can get in through the kitchen at the back." Still holding Melissa, he fumbled in his pocket and held out a key to Jackson.

"Right. Come along." Jackson firmly shepherded all of them towards the gate. "I presume there's somebody else in the house. You have a babysitter of course?"

"Yes," said Michael. "She's probably watching television," he added irrelevantly.

Once inside the house Melissa rushed upstairs to the sleeping Rebecca.

"You'd better go with her, Canon," said Jackson. "Miss Davy, will you go to the babysitter please? Just tell her there's been an accident and we want her to stay here for a while. Mr Maltravers, you check through the house — don't go near the front door — and see if there's anything untoward. If there is, don't touch anything. I'm going to phone for a Panda car immediately but then I'll have to wait outside until they arrive."

Tess visibly pulled herself together and went through to the living-room.

"It's a woman's hand, isn't it?" said Maltravers.

"I didn't have time to see," Jackson replied briefly. "Where's the phone?"

Punt Yard was empty as Jackson returned to the front door and examined the grisly object upon it. The hand was fixed palm downwards with a six-inch nail penetrating between the metacarpal bones into the green painted wood; most of the nail was still protruding. There was surprisingly little evidence of blood. Anyone could have walked past the door without necessarily noticing the hand in the shadow, but its position over the lock made it impossible for anyone entering the house to miss it.

Only a few minutes passed before he heard an approaching police siren whose notes rose in intensity before the vehicle, its light flashing, appeared round the corner into the yard. The two officers told Jackson that Madden had been informed and was on his way. He left them on guard at the door then returned into the house where the others had gathered in the lounge with Jenny, the babysitter, an overweight and vacuous looking teenager whose face was fighting a scattered and spasmodic battle with acne. Jackson spoke first to Melissa.

"Is your little girl all right?" She nodded. "Did you find anything, Mr Maltravers?" He shook his head. "I imagine you all need a drink. I can't because I'm now on duty. Detective Chief Superintendent Madden is on his way. As this will be Mr Madden's inquiry, we had better wait until he arrives."

Jenny's startled and inquisitive eyes were scanning them, picking up the vibrations of their shock.

"What's goin' on?" she demanded. "I told me mum I'd be straight home and she'll be gettin' worried."

"I'm afraid there's been an accident," said Jackson.

"That's what Miss Davy said. What sort of accident?"

"Did you hear anything during the evening?" Jackson asked. "A bang or something?"

Jenny shook her head slowly. "No. What sort of a bang?"

"As though somebody knocked hard on the front door."

"No."

"The television was on, of course?"

"Yes. That was all right wasn't it Mrs Cowan?"

"Of course it was Jenny," said Melissa. "This gentleman is a policeman. He just has to find certain things out."

"Surely we can tell Jenny what's happened," said Michael.

"I'm afraid I can't allow that, sir," said Jackson.

"Good God, you're not suggesting . . . ?"

"I'm not suggesting anything, sir, but this is a police matter and I must ask you for your complete co-operation. Perhaps you could telephone this young lady's mother and say she's all right and you will get her home as soon as possible. Just say there's been an accident. Nothing more."

"As you wish," said Michael tersely. "I'll use the phone in the study."

"Mr Maltravers, would you come through to the kitchen with me for a moment please?" said Jackson. "I'd just like a private word."

"I'm coming as well," said Tess firmly. Jackson glanced at her for a moment then nodded his agreement.

"I think it's only fair to tell you," Jackson began when they had left the living-room, "that as far as I can make out it appears to be the hand of a young woman."

"Oh, my God," said Tess.

"I know what you must be thinking," Jackson continued. "All I can say is that it would be premature to jump to any conclusions before we have some definite evidence. I'm afraid we'll just have to wait until Mr Madden arrives. Until he's here my hands are tied . . ." Jackson stopped suddenly and closed his eyes. "I'm sorry . . . that wasn't the best way of putting it. You know what I mean. Let's just go back and join Mr and Mrs Cowan."

They all sat in uncomfortable silence for about ten minutes before they heard another car draw up and the sound of a voice directing someone to the garden gate.

"That's Mr Madden," said Jackson. "Just wait here for a moment."

Jackson met Madden in the kitchen and explained what he had done. Madden listened without making any interruption.

"Very well," he said finally. "I collected the police surgeon on

70

the way here and he's outside at the moment. You noticed that it's a woman's hand I take it?"

"Yes, sir."

"So it looks as though we might have found at least part of Miss Porter."

"That's the obvious conclusion, sir."

"I'm glad you agree with me this time," Madden said tersely. "I've told the car to radio for every available man to start house to house inquiries. Neale is on his way here as well and can help take statements. Where are the others?"

Madden glanced disapprovingly at the drinks when he entered the living-room. He was brusque, efficient, cold and detached and they were too shocked to protest. It was the start of a growing nightmare and they were all being helplessly swept into it.

Jackson himself took Maltravers' statement. No, he had seen nothing suspicious. The Yard had been full of cars when they left for the cathedral, but it obviously would be. Yes, he was positive the hand had not been on the door when they set off. No, there had been no phone calls, no letters.

"I'd have bloody well told you that," he snapped.

"I know. But we need everything for a formal statement. I know I've asked you this before, but do you know of any threats that have been made against Miss Porter?"

Maltravers looked up. "It is Diana's hand then?"

"Until we know otherwise, it's a possibility we have to consider," Jackson replied evenly.

Maltravers took out a cigarette, lit it and exhaled the smoke slowly.

"What you are asking me to accept," he began quietly, "is that somebody has cut off Diana's hand and nailed it to the god-damned door!" His voice ended in a near shout. "I don't want to know that!"

Jackson remained very quiet for a moment while Maltravers stared at the floor.

"Do you know of anyone who has made threats against Miss Porter?" he repeated, quietly.

Maltravers shook his head without looking up again. "No. And I wasn't shouting at you."

71

"I know that. It doesn't matter. I'm sorry, I can't think of anything to say." Jackson got to his feet and held out his hand. "I'll still try to keep you informed."

"Thank you," said Maltravers and they shook hands. "What happens next?"

"The hand has been photographed where it was found and taken to the mortuary." Maltravers winced at the word. "Look," Jackson continued hastily, "I know this is difficult for you, but obviously fingerprints will produce the answer very quickly. We could find something in Miss Porter's flat but that will take time. Is there anything here which only she is likely to have touched? Something in her room?"

Maltravers took him upstairs to Diana's room where Jackson saw a bedside lamp with a smooth, glazed pottery base. He unplugged it from the wall, put a handkerchief on the edge of the shade and carefully lifted it.

"Theoretically, this should be perfect," he said. "It's unlikely that anyone else touched it after her arrival and I imagine your sister cleaned everything beforehand. I'll let you know what we find out."

Jackson returned to the police station where he was told that Madden was with the police surgeon in the mortuary next door. He found them together, the surgeon a Scot broad in shoulder and accent whose Harris tweed sports jacket smelt as if woven out of tobacco leaf. The hand lay between them on a stainless-steel-topped table.

"You'll perceive it's a woman's hand," the surgeon was saying. "It would be a most extraordinary man who kept his fingernails in that condition." The nails were finely manicured and glistening with a faint silver varnish.

"Anyway," the surgeon continued, "if you're going to argue that some men have funny habits, they don't get pregnant as well."

"Pregnant?" snapped Madden. "How can you tell?"

"Look here." The surgeon lifted the hand and pointed to a tiny red dot with fine lines running from it about two millimetres across. "Spider naevus. They appear after about three months." He turned the hand so they could see the ends of the wrist bones.

"From the condition of the radius and the ulna, I'd estimate someone in her early to mid-twenties but X-rays might throw more light on that. There's no pitting of the nails, so she didn't suffer from psoriasis and, for what it's worth, she wasn't a mongol. The palm creases for that are unmistakable."

"How was the hand cut off?" asked Madden.

"Not by a skilled surgeon at any rate. The bones are cut clean through and, if you want a guess, I would suggest a meat cleaver or something similar. It certainly wasn't sawn off."

"Was she alive when it was done?"

The surgeon shrugged. "That's difficult. Most of the blood has flowed out, which might indicate that she was alive or it had been done very soon after death, while the blood was still fluid. But the clotting process is reversed after a while by bacterial activity which makes the blood fluid again. I can't say anything else until I've done more tests."

"Thank you, doctor," said Madden. "Before that, we'll want to take fingerprints though. See to it will you, sergeant?"

"Yes, sir. I've brought this from the house." Jackson held up the bedside lamp and explained. Madden grunted with qualified approval.

"That should save time," he acknowledged. "Let me know the results immediately."

Jackson waited while Higson, his vocabulary reduced to virtual silence by being called from his bed, checked the lamp with prints taken from the hand. After peering intently at the results for a few moments, he looked up.

"Yes," he said briefly. "Anything else?"

Jackson shook his head and Higson packed up without a further word and left. Jackson returned the hand to the mortuary then went back to the police station. As he walked along the corridor to Madden's office he passed an open door on which a sign saying "Incident Room" had been newly fixed. Inside he could see filing cabinets and telephones being put into place and there was a tangible air of activity emanating from it; William Madden was in his element again.

In his own office, the Chief Superintendent heard with evident

73

satisfaction that the fingerprints proved it was Diana's hand; it was not yet a murder but it was a crime of eminently satisfying seriousness.

"The other line of investigation, of course, is the father of the child," he said when Jackson had finished. "Mr Maltravers, perhaps?" His silence and narrowed eyes invited Jackson to follow him down an avenue of thought.

"Mr Maltravers has a girlfriend, sir. Miss Davy. I think his relationship with Miss Porter was a professional one with no more than ordinary friendship." Jackson was declining to take even the first step. The possibility that Maltravers might be the father of Diana's child was a link in the chain of Madden's mind; sex and murder, like love and hate, were common companions.

"In any case, sir, even if he were the father, he certainly could not have nailed the hand on the door. He was with three other people when he left the house and for most of the evening I was with him. We all left the cathedral together and I was only a few feet behind him when we discovered the hand. He's one of quite a number of people who can be ruled out."

Madden pondered the point.

"You're sure he never left you?" Jackson nodded. "Then . . . the question is, did whoever nailed that hand to the door choose his moment because he knew they were all out of the house? In which case he either saw them leave . . . or saw them in the cathedral and left before they did."

"Both are possible," said Jackson. "A great many people left before we did."

Madden pinched his nose, then shook his head briskly.

"A great many holes, sergeant. We'll need a lot more evidence yet." The phone on his desk rang. "Right," he said after listening for a moment, then rang off. "The incident room is ready. Come with me for the initial briefing then I want you to go back to Punt Yard and tell them it is Miss Porter's hand. And see if they can throw any light on the father of the child. This way."

With his customary efficiency, Madden had organised nearly twenty officers in the incident room which was already virtually fully equipped to deal with the anticipated mass of information

74

which would eventually come in. Jackson joined the rest and they sat or stood in a rough semi-circle as Madden spoke.

"First of all, it has been established that the hand discovered earlier this evening is that of Diana Porter, the actress who disappeared on Sunday," he began. "Inquiries into her disappearance have yielded nothing so far. As you know, I've already ordered checks to be made with all hospitals and doctors in the immediate area to see if they have treated anyone for a severed hand. These inquiries will be extended to other forces if necessary.

"At present this is obviously not a murder inquiry but until we find that she has received medical treatment it will be regarded as one, body or no body." Madden turned to where a hastily blown-up map of the area immediately surrounding the cathedral had been pinned to the wall and pointed to a red sticker.

"This is where she was last seen in the Dean's garden at about six o'clock on Sunday afternoon. The hand was discovered on the door of Canon Cowan's house here, about a hundred yards away. Not a great many people live in the immediate area but there are a lot of tourists passing through it. Every home is to be visited. I want notices put up here, here . . . and here." He indicated the entrance from the main road into Punt Yard, the alleyway that ran from the north transept to the city centre shops and a point outside the Chapter House. "People who have been there in the past couple of days may visit again and I want them interviewed. Anything suspicious. Anyone behaving strangely. Anyone even remotely answering Miss Porter's description. Sergeant Neale has arranged enlargements of the photographs issued to the press when she went missing.

"I'm detailing officers to make inquiries in London. This woman had a great many friends in the acting profession. I want everything they know. Any threats, professional jealousies. And, most important, boyfriends. She was pregnant." His tone implied no moral condemnation, although he was known to be puritanical in such matters; in these circumstances, Diana's pregnancy was nothing more than a line of investigation.

"Her only known relative is a brother and the police in Bristol will be talking to him." He looked round the attentive group.

"Any questions? Right. Keep in constant touch with this room. Inspector Barratt will be in day-to-day charge. I've arranged a press conference for first thing in the morning. I don't like newspapers but publicity may be of assistance." Madden's icy gaze swept his audience again. "Don't waste time. Follow procedures. I want results." He turned towards the door. "All leave cancelled," he added and left the room.

It was gone midnight when Jackson returned to Punt Yard but there was still a light showing from the living-room window. He spoke briefly to the constable Madden had left stationed outside the house, then rang the bell. While he was waiting for someone to come to the door, he looked at the nail hole above the lock. It was quite shallow; obviously whoever it was had risked only one quick blow to avoid unnecessary noise. Michael opened the door and led him through to where the others were gathered with their shock. His look erased any lingering hopes they had been clinging to.

"I'm very sorry," he said. "It is Miss Porter's hand."

Melissa put her face into her hands and began to weep as Tess, her features contorted with controlled grief, slipped her arm around Maltravers.

"We're grateful to you for coming to tell us, sergeant," Michael said quietly. "This must be very difficult for you as well."

"Thank you, Canon," said Jackson. "There is something else as well which we need to know about. Did Miss Porter tell you she was going to have a baby?"

They stared at him. "How the hell . . . ?" Maltravers began.

"There was something about the hand which showed it. I can't remember the word the police surgeon used but it's definite. Miss Porter never mentioned it?"

"Not a word," said Maltravers. "But it does explain her relationship with Rebecca. I never noticed any signs though."

"Well, apparently, it might only have been about three months so it would not have been all that visible. But that was a very loose dress she wore at the Chapter House."

"Everything she wore was like that," added Tess.

"The question is, have you any idea who the father might be?" asked Jackson.

Tess and Maltravers looked at each other, then both shook their heads.

"Diana has plenty of boyfriends but none in particular as far as I know," said Maltravers.

"Very well. I won't trouble you further at the moment but if you do find anything about who it might be please let us know. I'm sorry to have had to tell you the worst news. We'll let you know as soon as anything happens. Goodnight." Jackson turned to leave the room, then paused. "Oh, just one other thing. The basic facts of what happened tonight are being released to the Press Association. I'm afraid you will find the publicity distressing but it may help us to find Miss Porter, which is the most important thing at the moment. It's all right, Canon, I'll let myself out."

As they heard the sound of Jackson closing the front door, Melissa lifted her eyes from the handkerchief which she had been crumpling between her fingers on her lap.

"I know you don't think much of this sort of thing, Augustus," she said, "but I'm going upstairs to say some prayers." She stood up and held out her hand to Michael. "Will you come with me please, darling?" They left the room together.

"Come and sit down," Tess said to Maltravers and he sat on the chair by the fireplace while she curled up at his feet holding his hand. For a few minutes he sat impassively then his face suddenly crumpled and he began to cry with a terrible adult intensity. Tess knelt up and put her arms around him, rocking him gently back and forth as tears streamed down her own cheeks.

In the incident room, Madden's team had checked with nearly forty hospitals, including most of the London ones. There were no reports of anyone being treated for a severed hand.

Chapter 7

REBECCA WOKE EARLY in the morning and the house was suddenly filled with childish laughter and demands and an unreal edge of normality as Press, television and radio reports exploded their private horror into public awareness. Just before nine o'clock Joe Goldman rang.

"Gus? I've heard. It's really true?"

"I'm afraid so. It was too late last night to call you. Sorry."

"Don't apologise. How's Tess? How are you? Hell, what sort of questions are those? Look, can I do anything?"

"The police will almost certainly want to see you. One thing they're obviously asking is if anyone ever made any threats against Diana. Do you know of anything?"

"Possibly. That's why I'm at the office early. I heard the radio first thing and remembered something and I've just been checking it. I think you'd better pass it on to them. You remember that *Hedda Gabler* business? Diana had a lot of fan mail after that, often asking for signed photographs. Most of the letters came through here. It was all a joke to her of course but she signed the pictures putting silly messages on most of them. I told her it was stupid but she insisted. Anyway one guy wrote back and it was a bit weird so I kept the letter. Listen to this.

" 'Dear Diana, I have received your signed photograph which I am keeping by my bed with the picture from the newspaper. I look at them both a lot and think a lot of things which I couldn't tell my mam about.' So we all know what he's doing in bed, don't we? But the next bit is worrying. 'I keep them with my razor sharp Commando's knife because they are the things I treasure most.' See what I mean?"

"Christ Almighty! Who is this character?"

"Arthur Powell, twenty-seven Sebastopol Terrace, Bels-thwaite. That's Yorkshire somewhere, isn't it?"

"It's near Halifax. All right, thanks Joe. I'll tell the police. I'm no detective, but don't handle that letter any more than you have to. They'll be checking it for fingerprints."

"Gus, did I do the wrong thing?" Anguish suddenly entered Goldman's voice. "I should maybe have told the police when it arrived. I mean, it was just a nutty letter. I never thought. Maybe if I'd . . ."

"Stop it, Joe!" Maltravers interrupted. "You weren't to know. What's important is that you kept the letter."

"But Gus, Diana's dead!"

"We don't know that. All we know is that she's been injured. Now just stay at the office and wait for the police to arrive."

Goldman's information was passed to Madden immediately Maltravers phoned it in. Madden had arranged for a camp-bed to be set up in his office for the occasional and inadequate periods of sleep he took during a major inquiry.

"You and Neale go to Belsthwaite at once," he told Jackson. "I'll contact the police there and have them hold Powell until you arrive. I want him back here at once."

As they left, Madden contacted the incident room and ordered a search of police central records for anyone called Arthur Powell and despatched a man to London to collect the letter from Goldman. He then rang the police in Belsthwaite and requested the immediate arrest of Arthur Powell on suspicion of kidnapping and assault occasioning grievous bodily harm.

"Let me know personally as soon as you have him," he said. "My men should be there by noon. They'll take over from there."

While the bleak northern thoroughfare of Sebastopol Terrace was suddenly filled with the wail of sirens and the screech of brakes as men leapt out of cars to hammer at a front door, Madden sat and quietly read a report from the Chief Constable on drug abuse in the county, his eyes narrowing at his superior's thoughts favouring the possible legalisation of cannabis and his mouth making a pout of distaste at the recorded reduction of fines and sentences; for twenty minutes neither Diana Porter nor

Arthur Powell entered his mind until the phone rang again with a return call from Belsthwaite. Arthur Powell could not be found.

Madden made brief notes on his pad as he listened to the flat Yorkshire narrative. Powell was not at home and inquiries at the supermarket where he worked in the stock room revealed that he had gone on holiday the previous Friday. Nobody knew where but it was believed he had gone camping. A description of his motor cycle and sidecar would be sent to Vercaster as soon as possible and further inquiries were being made with neighbours and the supermarket staff.

"Inform sergeants Jackson and Neale when they arrive," Madden said. "All further reports to go directly to the incident room. Thank you for your assistance."

He walked from his office to the incident room itself and crisply reported what he had been told to the officer collating information, then turned irritatedly to an Inspector from the public relations department.

"What is it?" he snapped.

"The Press, sir. The conference was due to begin ten minutes ago."

Madden made no comment but picked up the latest summary of the situation from the desk in front of him.

"Five minutes," he said and, as he rapidly digested the current information which contained nothing of significance except what he already knew about Powell, composed his mind to deal with the Press.

When he entered the conference room exactly five minutes later he was businesslike but cordial. Ignoring the statement which had been prepared before the information came in about Powell, he outlined the case in spare, clear sentences finishing with the news of what was happening in Belsthwaite.

"We are seeking a man called Arthur Powell who we have reason to believe may be able to help us with our inquiries," he said baldly. He did not reveal the address or anything about Powell's letter to Diana. When it was clear he had finished, a barrage of questions erupted around the room.

"I will only take questions one at a time," he said sternly. "The gentleman at the front."

"Chief Superintendent, who is this man Powell? What is his connection with Diana Porter?"

"We're not certain. We only know that he wrote to her."

"What did the letter say?"

"We can't reveal that at present."

Calmly and methodically, Madden continued to stonewall, producing an amazing series of variations on "No comment". Personal questions about Diana could not be answered; the Press would have to inquire elsewhere. No (this with the slightest facial flicker of contempt for the questioner) it would not be possible to take a picture of the severed hand. No (this with an air of genuine regret) there were no pictures of Powell at present but these would be supplied as soon as possible if he was not traced. Yes (this with an edge of diffident acknowledgement) he was the officer in charge of the investigation. Madden with two d's, first name William. No (and this must be clearly understood) he was not conducting a murder inquiry.

"All we are certain of is that Miss Porter is missing and that she has received a very serious injury. We are very anxious to trace her and have reason to believe Mr Powell may be able to assist us in this. We will, of course, be very grateful for any assistance you can give in the way of publicity. I'm sorry but I can add nothing more at this stage but you will be informed of any significant developments. Thank you for your co-operation."

The Press were far from satisfied but Madden's intention was to use them, not accommodate them. But they had more than enough to go on. The bloody happenings at Punt Yard connected with a beautiful and well-known actress were rich and delectable to the insatiable appetites of the front page and the screen. As knots of gossiping women gathered in Belsthwaite, as Maltravers sat with his growing aches of fear, as Vercaster went about its business, as the machinery of the police rolled relentlessly on, the slick and predictable phrases, occasionally enlivened by an imaginative adjective or dramatic observation, began to gather and form.

"Police are hunting the butcher who has savagely maimed actress Diana Porter . . . a city is living in terror after a mangled and mutilated hand was found cruelly nailed to a door in the

81

shadow of its cathedral . . . there are fears for the life of one of Britain's most dazzling talents . . . one terrible question is haunting the police — will Diana's other hand be found? . . . people knelt and prayed in Vercaster Cathedral today for a beautiful young woman they had grown to love . . . Diana Porter is the helpless, terrified prisoner of a monster . . . London's theatre world was shattered today by the news that . . ." With the facts they had at their disposal, the most prosaic of journalistic talents could work wonders.

Maltravers agreed to speak to the Press on behalf of everyone at Punt Yard, controlling his feelings and keeping his patience even when one reporter asked for the spelling of *Hedda Gabler*. They pressed him relentlessly about Diana's pregnancy — which Madden had mentioned — demanding what he knew about her boyfriends. Having convinced them that he was certainly not one, he was unable to offer any suggestions.

"What about this guy Powell?" one asked.

"Well he certainly wasn't a boyfriend. As far as I know, Diana didn't even know him." Jackson had passed on specific instructions from Madden that he was to say nothing about Powell beyond the police statement.

"Did he cut off her hand?"

"I don't know. Ask the police."

"Come on, we've tried that. They're not saying. Give us a break on this."

"They're not saying because they don't know!" Maltravers, his patience rapidly vanishing, looked hard at the journalists gathered round the front step of Punt Yard. "I don't give a damn who cut off Diana's hand. It's been done. And I'm more interested in finding her than in who did it. Anybody who cares for Diana just wants her found and given proper medical treatment. We're grateful for the coverage you've given to the fact that she went missing. Now, for God's sake try to help find her!"

In Belsthwaite, Jackson and Neale were coming to the conclusion that they were hunting an invisible man. Powell had worked at the supermarket for three years without making any friends either there or among his neighbours in Sebastopol Terrace. He was quiet, efficient, unambitious and colourless. His flat, when they entered it, was bleak and functional, the furniture belonging to the landlord with little to reveal anything about the tenant's personality. There were no pictures or posters on the wall, no personal letters from family or friends. There was a collection of paperback books but the mixture of war novels, science fiction and thrillers was the sort that anyone might casually accumulate. There were also two books on health foods. In a drawer Jackson found a collection of large-scale Ordnance Survey maps of Wales and the West Country with dates going back several years written on various remote locations. As he examined them Neale made a grunt of discovery, having reached under the bed and pulled out a cheap plastic suitcase which contained several photograph albums each filled with colour prints, taken with little or no sense of composition, of desolate countryside. Under each one was written a location and a year. Borrowdale, 1973. Exmoor, 1974. Sutherland, 1975. The chronology jumped a couple of years then picked up again without any discernible pattern until Snowdonia the previous summer. They compared the photographs with the annotated maps and found they tallied. All the locations were for remote parts of Britain.

"Look at this," Jackson said. He had opened the last album to reveal more photographs, this time of Scandinavia, dated 1976 and 1977, the missing years from the previous albums. "He could be abroad then," he commented. "Let's see if there's a passport anywhere."

There was no sign of one nor indeed of any official communications apart from some brief correspondence with the Department of Social Security for a period of illness some six months previously and an envelope containing Powell's pass book for the Halifax Building Society with just over eleven hundred pounds in the account. The deposits had been a regular ten pounds a week with only major withdrawals of about £200 each July, tying in with the dates of his holidays.

"He's two dimensional," said Jackson. "I always worry with people like this. It makes you wonder what the other dimension is." As he spoke, that dimension, or at least something suggesting it, was emerging.

Belsthwaite police had taken Powell's fingerprints—there was only one set anywhere in the flat — and had checked with criminal records. The result was waiting for Neale and Jackson when they returned to Belsthwaite police station. Twenty years earlier, Arthur Powell had been jailed in his native South Wales for attempted rape with violence and had used a knife on the girl he had attacked. There was also a message from Madden that they were to return to Vercaster immediately.

By the time they got back, Madden had received a full report on Powell. The attack had been on a neighbour's sixteen-year-old daughter when he was living with his parents in a mining village near Swansea. He had given himself up and made a full confession, claiming that he had only used the knife to frighten her and had cut her in the neck when she started screaming. He had been jailed for six months during which he was a model prisoner and had undergone psychiatric treatment. The psychiatrist's report told of a markedly introverted character with difficulties over relationships with women. His father was a miner who had been pensioned off after contracting pneumoconiosis. This had caused the family financial difficulties resulting in his mother becoming a hostess at a Swansea nightclub, supplementing her income by casual prostitution. But the report noted that she had remained loyal to her husband, who had colluded with her activities, and the truth had been kept from the boy Arthur. Only when the psychiatrist had pushed him towards acknowledging what had been happening did he show any hostility, totally rejecting the suggestion about his mother as offensive and ridiculous. So extreme had his rejection been that the report concluded he had known the truth but refused to accept it. He had never married and there was no evidence that he was homosexual. Since that experience, Powell had apparently gone totally within himself, taking various unskilled jobs in different parts of Britain, always merging with the background and leaving no trace when he moved on. He had allowed nobody to come close to him.

There was one other development before Jackson and Neale reached Vercaster. The Belsthwaite police obtained a picture of Arthur Powell taken at the retirement of the previous supermarket manager and wired it down to the Vercaster incident room. Madden was examining it when they reported to his office.

"On the extreme left," he said and handed the photograph to them.

It showed an overweight, totally bald man in the centre, smiling ridiculously and holding an automatic tea-maker in a most unnatural pose, surrounded by about a dozen men and women in supermarket uniforms. Powell was standing towards the back, somehow giving the impression that he would have preferred not to be in the picture. Jackson looked at the face closely: pinched, narrow, furtive, expressionless amid smiles. Mentally he tried to stop selecting the adjectives which would fit the suspicions, but it remained a face which created a sense of unease. And there was something familiar about it.

"Copies are being issued in time for this evening's main television news," Madden continued. "In the meantime, take one round to Punt Yard and see if anyone there recognises him."

"Yes, sir." Jackson paused and looked at the picture again, frowning. "It's just that . . . I think I know him . . . I think . . ." He shook his head.

"Know him?" snapped Madden.

"I've got the feeling I've seen him. In Vercaster. But I can't remember where."

"Take it to Punt Yard," said Madden. "Perhaps it will come back to you." There was the slightest edge in his voice indicating that he expected it to.

The recollection remained frustratingly elusive as Jackson drove to Punt Yard and he sat in the car outside the house for several minutes vainly chasing it, an image in the corners of his memory. Maltravers suddenly appeared by the car door.

"I saw you through the window," he said as Jackson stepped out. "Have you found him?"

"I'm afraid not," said Jackson. "But I've got a picture I want you all to look at. I'll explain inside."

They listened in silence to Jackson's news, then he handed them the photograph without indicating which one was Powell.

"Just tell me if there's anyone you recognise," he said.

"Him." Maltravers and Melissa spoke instantly and together and then looked at each other in surprise.

Jackson stood up and took the picture back. "Which one are you referring to, Mrs Cowan? The man on the left. Mr Maltravers? The man on the left. Very well. Mrs Cowan, when and where have you seen him?"

"He was at the reception after Diana's performance. Don't you remember Augustus, I said he was staring in a funny way? But you didn't see him! He'd gone when you turned round. How do you recognise him?"

"Because I saw him the following day," replied Maltravers. "He was the chap staring at the house when we set off for the Dean's garden party. But you weren't with me then so you didn't see him."

"Are you both positive?" asked Jackson. They nodded their heads. "Very well, so Arthur Powell was in Vercaster on Saturday evening . . ." He stopped and snapped his fingers. "And that's where I saw him! In the Refectory! I'm sorry but I deliberately hadn't told you I thought I had seen him somewhere. And you say he was still here on Sunday afternoon."

"And now he's disappeared," said Maltravers. "Just like Diana."

For a moment all five of them were silent, reflecting on the implications of what had emerged.

"May I use your telephone, Canon?" said Jackson. "I want to speak to Mr Madden. Thank you."

Jackson could mentally see Madden making his precise notes as he related what had happened.

"Did you notice anything strange about his behaviour in the Refectory?" Madden asked when he had finished.

"Not really. It was just that he was one of the few people there who seemed to be on their own, talking to nobody, and that made him catch my eye."

"Take statements. Establish the times. Report back to me as soon as you return." Madden rang off abruptly.

The statements were brief, neither Melissa nor Maltravers having taken any great notice of Powell. Maltravers remembered he wore a checked shirt but was vague about the colour.

86

"And he was staring at this house?" said Jackson.

"Yes, but I expect a lot of people do. It's Georgian and tourists look at Georgian houses. When Tess said that was probably what he was I didn't think about it again."

"If you recall anything else, let us know," said Jackson and looked perceptively at their concerned faces. "I realise that this is not making things any better for you. Believe me, we're doing all we can to find Powell but he seems to have a habit of taking his holidays in remote places and if he is hiding somewhere he knows the sort of places to go. But don't worry, we'll find him."

"And Diana?" asked Maltravers quietly.

"I hope we can find her first," said Jackson. "We still have no reports of her being treated for her injuries but that doesn't mean it's not been done."

"No body, no murder," Maltravers said cynically.

Tess closed her eyes. "Shut up, Gus," she said and Jackson felt the vibrations of raw emotions breaking through the surface of their calm.

"I realise the worst thing is not knowing," he said as he stood up to leave. "Believe me we'll keep you fully informed. I'll see to that."

"Thank you, sergeant," said Melissa. "We're very grateful. We're going to the string quartet concert this evening so that may help to take our minds off things."

"The festival is still going ahead then?"

"Yes. The Dean came to see us today and wanted to cancel it but my brother insisted we should carry on. Most of our events have completely sold out and, as he said, Diana would want things to continue." Melissa smiled at Maltravers. "And we think it's best that we are seen to behave as normally as possible. We're being . . . very British. It's silly, but it's one way of getting through."

Decent behaviour was observed in the Chapter House that evening as well, the room tangibly tense, the audience speaking in whispers and averting their eyes away from the group to which they were irresistibly drawn, the musicians sombre, the applause polite but muted. There was another gathering in the Refectory afterwards with strained good manners polluting the air until it had the quality of poisoned jelly. The Dean apologised for the Bishop's absence.

"He's taking this very badly," he explained. "I don't need to tell you how impressed and attracted he was by Miss Porter. He asked me to convey his greatest sympathy. My wife and I feel a sense of responsibility as well. Miss Porter was a guest in our home and if we had taken greater notice, then . . ."

"That's very kind but quite unnecessary, Dean," Maltravers interrupted. "There was nothing any of us could have done."

Affected by the atmosphere, people began leaving early and Maltravers and Tess were preparing to follow them when he felt the sleeve of his jacket plucked. It was Miss Targett.

"Oh, Mr Maltravers," she began and tears sprang to her eyes as she overcame the obstacle of speech. "This is a very, very wicked thing. Miss Porter was so . . ." Her kindly little face suddenly shivered into grief and Maltravers swallowed hastily as her emotion caught him.

"Thank you, Miss Targett," he said. "We do appreciate your feelings."

"But she was your friend!" Miss Targett's voice cried with simple anguish. "Such a dear, kind, lovely girl . . ." She began to sob helplessly and Maltravers and Tess gazed in embarrassment, unable to find anything to do or say in comfort. They were saved by the arrival of Webster, the Succentor, who put his arm round the old lady.

"Come along, Miss Targett," he said gently. "Let me take you through to the Lady Chapel for a few minutes." As she turned with childlike obedience, he smiled slightly at Tess and Maltravers to indicate he would handle things and walked away with his arm still about Miss Targett's shoulders.

"It's not just us, is it?" said Tess as they watched them go. "There are all sorts of people being hurt by this. The Bishop, Melissa and Michael, Miss Targett. All those people who identify with the famous. Even the Dean's wife. Dear God, let Diana be found soon."

Chapter 8

THE STING OF Miss Targett's distress and the image of her cheerful and animated face distorted by horror moved restlessly about Maltravers' mind all through the night. The Dean's feelings of responsibility added irrational echoes. It was Maltravers who had brought Diana to Vercaster, the archetypal cathedral city where bad things did not happen. The feeling began to grow in him that he could not just allow things to go on without trying to do something. As morning light seeped through the bedroom curtains he lay and stared at them.

"Are you awake?" Tess's arm stretched across his body.

"I can't remember being asleep. There's something Hardy wrote — in *The Mayor of Casterbridge* I think — about there being an outer compartment to the mind into which terrible thoughts come uninvited. Mine's very over-occupied at the moment."

"I know. I keep trying to tell myself the reality won't be as bad. But I don't believe myself."

"I'm going to Belsthwaite," he said.

Tess raised her head. "Belsthwaite? Why?"

"Because I might find something out. Because it's something to *do*."

"The police are doing everything they can."

"I know that, but I just might . . . I don't know . . . I might find something they've missed. Perhaps someone will talk to me because I'm not a policeman. Perhaps . . . I can't just stay here and do nothing."

Tess looked at him for a moment. "All right. But I'm coming with you. Don't argue. You're not the only one who needs something to do."

Maltravers did not argue or even reply but put his arm around Tess and pulled her closer to him. They lay in silence until they heard the sound of the morning paper arriving through the letter box.

Arthur Powell's thin face, slightly blurred after being enlarged from the original photograph, stared impassively from the grey columns of the *Daily Telegraph*. Maltravers stood in the hall reading the accompanying story, a cold informative narrative, inevitably detached from the reality of the experience. There was a description of Powell's vehicle — like himself it was nondescript — and a warning from the police that he should not be approached. The story added that he had been seen in Vercaster at the weekend but the official position was still that he was wanted for nothing more specific than to assist with police inquiries. Maltravers suddenly found the iron laws which curtailed reporting in such circumstances slightly absurd. The suspicions against Powell were overwhelming and his disappearance a tacit confirmation of his guilt, which would be increasingly reinforced the longer he failed to come forward. At the end of the story about Powell was a separate short piece about the Latimer Mercy which included a quote by Madden that the police were not connecting the incidents.

Over breakfast Maltravers told Melissa what he and Tess planned to do.

"I can't see what you'll achieve," she said. "But I can't see what anything will achieve. Michael's taking Rebecca to his parents in Sussex for a few days and will stay overnight but I'll be here to take any messages."

"You'll be all right on your own?"

"Yes. Don't worry. I've got people coming round. You'll be back tonight?"

"Of course, but it might be late. We'll call you before we set off. And we'd better get going now."

Their departure was delayed by a telephone call from Joe Goldman.

"Have they found this bastard yet?" he demanded.

"Not as far as we know and I'm sure they'd be in touch with us if they had. How are things with you?"

90

"You wouldn't believe it, Gus. It's death in the family time. I've had grown men crying on the phone."

"Joe, there's no proof Diana's dead."

"You said that before but what comfort is it that she might be alive with her godammed hand cut off? Sorry, Gus, I know it must be worse for you but this is getting to a lot of people here. Anyway, that's not why I called. There's something worrying me and I wanted to talk to you about it."

"About Powell?"

"No something else. It doesn't make much sense but I can't stop thinking about it. Do you remember Peter Sinclair? He was in *Success City*."

Maltravers had to think a moment before Sinclair, an actor with the facial looks of an Action Man toy whose conceit far outweighed his talent, came back to him. His part in the trilogy had been a minor one; he died halfway through the first episode.

"What about him?"

"You know he and Diana had an affair? Nothing serious for her, she was just playing the field, but he really got in deep. When she finished it he became the classic rejected lover, flowers, phone calls, the lot. If you met him all he talked about was Diana. Anyway, the next thing is he's going into hate, stupid threats that he'll get even. You wouldn't believe what he was like. You remember that cat Diana had?"

"Who doesn't? She was besotted with the thing. It disappeared, didn't it?"

"Yes . . . and a couple of days later its tail was pushed through her letter box. Next thing is Sinclair's saying he's had his revenge. The guy's a weirdo, Gus."

"Did she ask him about the cat?"

"He just laughed it off. But you see what I'm thinking? There's only one problem. He's in California."

"California! Since when?"

"About three months ago. He landed a part as an English chauffeur in some new American TV soap opera."

"Come on, Joe, you know what those shooting schedules are like. How does he find time to get back to England?"

"I don't know. It just keeps nagging me. If he did cut up the cat he's nutty enough for anything."

"Just a minute. When was this affair? When did it end?"

"It started when they were shooting *Success City*. When was that? Just over a year ago. It lasted about three months. Why?"

"It's all right, it doesn't fit. You knew Diana was pregnant?"

"Yes, I read it in the paper . . . Oh, I see what you're driving at. No, it can't have been him. She'd have had it by now."

"Any idea who it might have been? The father?"

Goldman grunted down the phone. "No one comes to mind. She was kicking around with two or three guys but there was nothing serious as far as I know."

"OK, Joe, thanks for telling me about Sinclair. I'll keep in touch."

"Do that, Gus. Love to Tess, you know? A lot of people have asked me to say that."

Maltravers thought over what Joe had told him as they prepared to leave for Belsthwaite. The continuous pattern of rehearsals and shooting for a long-running series left nobody any time to get away and there would probably be contractual limitations on Sinclair's movements as well. But he still decided the police should know. He called Goldman back to ask the name of the studios, then called Jackson.

"I take your point that it seems highly unlikely," Jackson said when he had finished. "But we'll check it out just in case. Incidentally, we've had the usual crop of reported sightings of Powell since his picture appeared but none has turned out to be him so far. It always happens. If he does turn up I'll call you as soon as I can."

"Thanks. Actually I won't be here for the rest of the day but my sister will be at home," Maltravers replied. "Tess and I are going to London."

Maltravers felt ridiculously guilty as they left Vercaster heading north, imagining that Jackson would see them and stop the car. He had no rational explanation for what they were doing; his reasons for going to Belsthwaite were deep, personal and irrelevant to everybody and everything except himself.

Belsthwaite lay in the remains of what must have been a beautiful Yorkshire dale, its lower reaches now savagely scarred by the merciless urban development spawned by the industrial explosion which had supported the world's last and greatest Empire. As they crested a hill it appeared below them, a dark sluggish river coiling out of its unlovely brickwork which climbed unevenly towards the tops of the valley ridges. A silent mill dominated one side of the town, long disused and with windows like tombstones staring blankly across the cramped back yards and alleyways of what had been the homes of its workers. On the opposite side of the river, post-war development had planted some newer industries and brighter houses scattered amid worn patches of green. Sebastopol Terrace, with its parallel companions of Inkerman, Balaclava and Crimea itself, instantly admitted its origins in far-away battlefields. The houses stood in long, stark rows like the very brigades they silently commemorated and the brilliant sun only served to exaggerate their bleakness.

Number twenty-seven was one of many which had been converted into upper and lower, obviously cramped, flats. There were no front gardens. The step up from the pavement was of porous sandstone, now leprous with age, and the narrow strip of diamond-shaped black and white tiles beyond it was cracked and discoloured. There were two doorbells, one unmarked and the other with a yellowing strip of paper beneath it, in a dirty clear plastic holder, bearing the name Powell.

"Not much point in trying that," said Maltravers and pressed the alternative. There was no sound.

"Does it work?" asked Tess.

"Who knows? Bells that you can't hear from outside are always infuriating."

They had discussed where they would start as they drove north, deciding that gossip of their visit would spread more quickly from the supermarket and might provoke police interest, which could interfere with calling in Powell's neighbourhood.

"Although asking questions is no offence in law," Maltravers had remarked.

"But it's not advisable when the police are involved," Tess had replied.

Maltravers peered through one of the matching mottled-glass panes in the front door, his hand cupped above his eyes.

"I think there's someone coming," he said and moments later the blurred outline of a figure became visible on the inside. After a fumbling of lock the door opened slightly and a face peered out suspiciously.

The resulting conversation became so bizarre that Maltravers later regretted that he did not have the opportunity to record it. Having established that they were not from the landlord, the council, or any one of several hire-purchase companies; were not social workers, Jehovah's Witnesses or itinerant sellers of any manner of goods; did not want to lend or borrow money; had no intention of offering cut-price decorating; did not wish to discuss the purchase of unwanted jewellery or other valuables; were not conducting any form of consumer survey; had no connection with Authority (particularly the police) in any way, shape or form; and meant, in short, no harm, expense or embarrassment, the occupier opened the door more fully to reveal himself as a man of advanced years and sullen manner with braces and a shirt without a collar.

"What do you want then?" he demanded.

"Well, actually, we're inquiring about your neighbour, Mr Powell," said Maltravers with the greatest amiability he could manage after so relentless a grilling.

"Don't know 'im," said the man and closed the door before even the fleetest foot could have stopped it. Maltravers, his mouth still open to continue what he had to say, stared in amazement and Tess suddenly giggled.

"We're not very good at this," she said.

"I've always thought they were mad in Yorkshire," said Maltravers. "This never happened to Lord Peter Wimsey."

"Perhaps not. But he never came to Belsthwaite."

Calls at the immediately adjacent houses were equally unprofitable. Nobody was at home in one case and at the other house there was a lady of remarkable deafness, a handicap made more difficult by the fact that she carried a perpetually yapping

Yorkshire terrier. Gesturing meaninglessly at her, Tess and Maltravers admitted defeat and returned to the car.

They were about to drive away when Tess pointed out a small corner shop at the end of the terrace, a surprising survivor of changing shopping habits. Maltravers said it would be little use as Powell would obviously buy his groceries at the supermarket where he was employed but Tess said she would try it.

"It's an obvious gossip mine," she said. "Since the publicity in the papers and on television everybody will be talking about Powell. You stay here and I'll go and have a chat."

"And what makes you think they'll talk to a complete stranger?" he asked.

"They'll talk to anybody. Particularly someone who talks broad Yorksheer. Rest thissen here lad, and I'll see what's oop." She stepped out of the car.

Maltravers watched her disappear into the shop, its tinny bell sounding outside in the street, and admiringly noticed that her long-legged walk gave the indefinable impression of being a Yorkshirewoman; good acting always starts with the feet. While he waited, he looked through all the morning papers they had bought on the motorway during the journey, following the irresistible urge to read again and again in print what they knew so well. The tabloid front pages contained little else but Powell's face, combining journalistic high drama and the desired effect of making it familiar to millions of readers. They also had pictures of Diana — showing some sense of restraint by not using the nude one — and had all reached for their most spectacular typefaces and emotive language. "Is this Diana's butcher?" screamed one headline, with cavalier disregard for possible libel actions should Powell unexpectedly turn out to be innocent, and all included excitable prose padded out with such strange irrelevances as the Vercaster District Council motto — "Serve God and people" — and the date of the Chapter House, variously given between eleventh and thirteenth centuries. Maltravers read them all, his occasional twitches of distaste counterbalanced by the awareness that they should hasten the discovery and arrest of Arthur Powell and, hopefully, the rescue of Diana; he clung, limpet-like, to the belief that she was still alive.

Tess returned after about twenty minutes carrying chocolate and crisps.

"I had to buy something," she said as she got back into the car. "And the only problem was stopping her talking. Powell bought his papers there and she's the sort who would make a Trappist monk speak. Most of it was just chit-chat but she's obviously been searching her memory since the police called. I had the feeling that she wasn't very happy about telling them too much. Apparently he always called in on Friday to pay his bill and last week said he was going on holiday. We know that, of course, but old Mrs Whatever-her-name-is asked him where he was going and he said he was off to spend a couple of days in London and then to the mountains."

"Just the mountains?"

"Unfortunately yes. Wales?"

Maltravers frowned. "Or the Lake District. Or Scotland. Or even abroad. Jackson told us they couldn't find his passport. Still it rules out some places like Devon and Cornwall which is something. I'll tell Jackson when we get back. Come on, let's try the supermarket."

They decided the only thing they could do was admit they were friends of Diana and hope for the best. As it turned out the new manager, eager and trying to hide his youth behind an immature moustache, was quite unconcerned that their inquiries were not official and took them straight through to his office, hauling assorted boxes off chairs so they could sit down.

"We still can't believe it," he said. "Nobody was really a friend of Arthur but nobody disliked him. He's the sort who wouldn't hurt a fly. Nobody here can ever remember him even losing his temper."

"Do you know anything about him? He seems indefinable."

Their conversation was interrupted by the manager being called to sort out a dispute on a check-out. When he returned he was accompanied by a stout, jolly woman whom he introduced as one of his supervisors. He explained the reason for Maltravers and Tess's visit.

"How would you describe Arthur, Mildred?" he asked her.

"Very close. Always polite, mind, but never used two words

96

where one were enough. Never gave change in conversation. Mind, you could say nowt against him. Only thing that sticks in my mind is he were faddy with his food."

"Faddy? What do you mean?"

"One of them vegetarians. I told 'im there were nowt worth eatin' in rabbit fodder but he were very particular. Wouldn't even eat a boiled egg sandwich and where's the harm in that?"

"Did you ever see him with a Commando knife?" asked Maltravers. Sudden recollection broke over Mildred's face.

"Ay, I'd forgotten that. One of them big things in a leather sheath. Now that were his pride and joy. Always had it with him and had one of those stone things for sharpening it on. He used to cut up the boxes in the storeroom with it." She frowned as she thought back. "Now I think about it, he seemed . . . I don't know . . . happy somehow when he were doing that."

Maltravers and Tess exchanged disturbed glances. After a few more minutes' conversation it became clear that neither Mildred nor the manager would recall anything else; Powell had kept himself to his secret self very carefully, even among the people with whom he worked.

As they were about to drive out of the car park, they heard a shout and saw the manager running towards them carrying something.

"I just remembered," he said as Maltravers wound down the car window. "Arthur always changed into these when he came to work. He kept them in the storeroom."

He held up a pair of cheap plastic sandals, cracked and worn with use.

"I suddenly thought, perhaps the police ought to have them." He looked at Maltravers, illogically seeking his approval.

"I expect it would be best," he replied. "Although I don't see how they can help. They've been through his flat. I suggest you give them a call. Thanks again for your help."

He pulled away and turned towards the town centre.

"Is there anywhere else we can try?" asked Tess.

"Not that I can think of. Oh, Christ, what a bloody waste of time! What on earth did we come for?"

"Because you needed to," said Tess quietly. "It has occupied your mind. Come on, let's find somewhere for lunch."

They found a town centre pub which served food and, while Tess was ordering at the bar, Maltravers rang Melissa.

"Augustus! Thank God you've called! How soon can you be back? Diana's other hand has been sent to the Dean through the post."

Chapter 9

AS THEY RETURNED south, they heard the news on the car radio. Melissa, her face drawn with shock, told them the details when they reached Punt Yard.

"It arrived in the second post," she said. "Just a small brown cardboard box addressed to the Dean."

"Was there any message?" Maltravers asked.

"No. It was just the hand. Apparently it was posted somewhere in London yesterday but the postmark is so smudged it's impossible to tell where. The police have got it now of course." Melissa suddenly threw her arms around her brother. "Oh, Augustus, this is so awful!" She began to weep. "The Dean's wife came round. She was so kind and you know what she's usually like. They want you to go and see them as soon as you can. The phone's never stopped with people saying all the right things and . . . and Michael's been on. And the Bishop. And the bloody Press. Augustus, they've got to find this dreadful man!"

Maltravers clung tightly to his strong, calm, capable, levelheaded sister, broken and battered by the terror that had invaded her orderly and certain world.

"Come on," he said. "We're back now. I'll take any more phone calls. Why don't you go down to Sussex?"

Melissa shook her head through her sobs. "No. It's better now you're both back and there's still the festival. I'm still being British however much it hurts. Stupid isn't it?"

"Yes," he said. "It's stupid. But the alternatives are stupider." He paused and frowned. "Stupider? Is there such a word? You know what I mean."

With excessive fastidiousness, Madden lifted the cardboard box with his fingertips, even though it had already been examined for

99

prints. One end bore the remains of a label showing that it had originally been used for packing bars of chocolates. Inside there was a dark-brown stain where blood had seeped into it. The gummed label bearing the Dean's name and address was typed.

"Sort of thing they have in supermarket stockrooms," he observed.

"Yes, sir," said Jackson. "Although they're not difficult for anyone to get hold of."

"And five sets of fingerprints."

"Yes. We've eliminated the Dean, of course, and Higson is at the Vercaster sorting office collecting prints from the postman and sorting clerks. The trouble is that it's impossible to say which office it went through in London at the moment. The lab's doing its best with the postmark but it looks fairly hopeless. What is certain is that we can't find Powell's prints on it. The best bet will be the saliva tests on the stamp and the label."

"Do we have saliva records of Powell?"

"No. But when we get him we'll be able to prove if he sent it."

Madden raised an eyebrow. "If?. Do we have any real alternatives?"

"There is this man Sinclair we now know about. We're still waiting to hear from Los Angeles."

"Long shot, sergeant. Very long." Madden was not to be diverted into investigating remote possibilities when Powell was fitting so exactly into the sort of pattern he liked best. "Any news about Powell?"

"We've had reports back from sightings in Borrowdale and the Peak District but they're negative. And there's still no trace of him having left the country."

"And still no reports of Miss Porter being treated for her injuries?" Jackson shook his head and a spasm of dissatisfaction tweaked across Madden's face; what was otherwise emerging as a very satisfactory investigation was hourly becoming closer to murder but still could not be neatly classified as such. He found that an annoying shortcoming as he contemplated the fugitive Powell trapped in a closing police net.

"And how's our Mr Maltravers?" he inquired mildly.

The unexpected polite and irrelevant question sounded instant alarm bells in Jackson's mind. Madden had dismissed his initial suspicions of Maltravers once Powell had appeared in the case and it was totally out of character for Madden to take any interest in him now.

"I haven't seen him today," he answered cautiously.

"Really? Where's he been?" There was the slightest suggestion of a cutting edge beneath the question this time and Jackson suddenly knew he was being led into dangerous ground.

"He told me he was spending the day in London, sir."

"And did he?"

"I presume so."

"You presume so. I see." Madden picked up the cardboard box and handed it back to Jackson. "If the lab have finished with that, have it labelled and filed. Thank you, sergeant." Jackson, aware he was caught in the coils of something he was ignorant about, but unable to make any comment, picked it up and turned to go as Madden started to read some of the papers on his desk.

"And I want Mr Maltravers — and Miss Davy — in this office within the next half hour," Madden added without looking up. Jackson turned back to ask a question but thought better of it.

He returned the box to the incident room and phoned Punt Yard from an empty office where he could not be overheard.

"What the hell have you been up to?" he demanded.

"Up to? What do you mean?"

"Madden wants to see you and Miss Davy immediately and he's playing games with me. He knows something I don't. Were you in London today?"

"Oh, that's what it is. Sorry. We went to Belsthwaite."

"You went to Belsthwaite." Jackson's voice was full of disappointment and resignation. "Do me one favour will you? Both of you come over here. Now. I've been giving you all the consideration I can and I'd like you to get me out of this."

They arrived at the police station within ten minutes and Jackson, without a word, took them through to Madden who was pedantically correct.

"I received a phone call at," he consulted his notepad, "fourteen seventeen hours today from the police authorities in Belsthwaite. They allege that two people fitting your descriptions and giving your names were making inquiries within their area of authority. These inquiries were in connection with a Mr Arthur Powell who, as you are fully aware, is the subject of an official police investigation in connection with the disappearance of Miss Diana Porter. Were these persons yourselves?"

"Yes," said Maltravers.

Madden nodded as if to himself. "I see. You are aware I take it that interference with the police in the course of their duties is an offence?"

"We weren't interfering. We thought it might possibly help."

"We thought it might possibly help." Madden wrote the remark down as he slowly repeated it. "I see. Do you have any comment to make Miss Davy?" Tess shook her head and Madden leaned back in his chair and regarded them thoughtfully.

"Despite the impression given by sensational fiction, the investigation of serious crime — of all crime — is a matter for the police," he said. "We do not seek, we do not require and we do not approve of interference — and that is what this is — by unqualified amateurs. Arthur Powell will be caught by the police and if your meddling today turns out to have caused any delay in this operation it will be noted in the official report on the matter. If it is repeated, the consequences for yourselves will be very serious indeed. That is all." Having delivered his lecture, Madden sat in silence waiting for them to leave. Jackson, acutely uncomfortable throughout, stiffly saluted Madden and turned to go but Maltravers remained in his chair.

"First of all, I wish to make it clear that neither Sergeant Jackson nor anyone in your force knew of our intention," he said. "In fact I deliberately lied to Sergeant Jackson this morning. Secondly, I can see no way in which what we did could be construed as interference. You obviously learned about this after the supermarket manager took a pair of Powell's sandals to the police in Belsthwaite, which was something I advised him to do. Had we learned anything of value that too would have been reported to your officers. Unless you can prove interference, then we have broken no law." His eyes, which had remained fixed on Madden's face, hardened. "So don't treat us like two bloody schoolkids who've been caught in the orchard with pockets full of apples! Your official investigation happens to concern the horrendous injuries and possible death by now of a very dear friend of ours and if there is anything I can do that I think might just possibly help to find her I am going to do it and you can stuff your regulations. And until and unless I break the law I am not going to be browbeaten by you or anybody else. Now you can make a note of that and add it to the goddammed file you've probably opened on me!"

Jackson's eyes were closed as though in prayer. Tess sat very upright and calm, her hands clasping her bag. Madden remained impassive. The silence gathered and froze about them.

"That will be all," Madden repeated stonily and this time Maltravers stood abruptly then stepped back to let Tess precede him out of the room with Jackson, who silently ushered them into an interview room.

"All I ask is one favour," he said. "Don't do that to me again. I deserve better."

"Madden started it, I finished it," snapped Maltravers.

"I'm not talking about just now. You lied to me and left me in an impossible position with a man who is my superior and with whom I have to work, whatever you think of him. Being as detached as I can in the circumstances, you were actually right in there. You haven't broken any law and you almost certainly haven't interfered with what we're doing. But I need a professional, working relationship with that man in the interests of solving crime. If you'd told me you were going to Belsthwaite, I'd have understood and I wouldn't have tried to stop you even if I could. But at least I'd have known and could have acted accordingly."

"You'd have told Madden."

"Let's just say I'd have covered myself. All you have achieved today is to make life difficult for me within weeks of joining this force. I don't care if you and Madden hate each other's guts but I have my career to think about." Jackson was biting with anger.

"Oh, I am his Highness's dog at Kew," Maltravers said savagely. "Pray tell me, Sir, whose dog are you?"

"If you two don't stop this instant, I am going to start screaming the place down." Tess's face was stiff with tension as they instinctively turned to her. Her voice began to break as she continued. "You do realise, don't you, that while you're both showing how macho you are, Diana is out there somewhere dying in agony? Christ, you make me sick." She started to cry angrily.

Her bitter accusation made them both wince uncomfortably and it was Jackson who began to retrieve the situation. He went over to Tess and took her hand.

"I'm sorry," he said. "We're both sorry. Murder — and whatever we say officially that's how we're all reacting to this — is like any form of violent death, like losing a wife or husband in a car crash. Until you face it, you cannot know what it's like. It stretches emotions beyond anything else that people have to face and if it happens you just have to hack it as best you can. And nobody goes through it without going out of control at some point."

"But you're not emotional," said Tess. "You're a policeman. It's just part of your job."

Jackson smiled sadly. "That's right. I'm a copper. Collecting clues, following procedures, enforcing the law. I'm not paid to be emotional." He paused for a moment then continued very quietly. "When I was sixteen years old my kid sister was raped and strangled. There's another thing about violent death. The scars never go away."

Tess swiftly wiped away fresh springing tears with her hand. "Oh, God, you're a lovely man," she said. Jackson squeezed her hand and stood up.

"That's another thing about detective stories," he said. "Have you ever noticed that hardly anybody cries? In real life, it's not just solving murders, it's people breaking up. Anyway, as you've been playing at detectives, did you find anything out?"

Maltravers shook his head. "No, we didn't. Oh, the sandals turned up." He briefly explained what had happened. "But I can't see they're going to help you. Look, I'm sorry we didn't tell you we were going but if we do do anything else — and I meant what I said to Madden — then I promise I'll let you know. And I'm sorry I got mad at you."

"That's all right. I think we understand each other a little better. Have you been to see the Dean? When I went there this morning I know he was very anxious to talk to you."

"We're going with Melissa after dinner," said Maltravers.

"Is she all right?"

"Coping." Maltravers pulled a wry face. "Like the rest of us."

Jackson escorted them back to the main entrance of the police station, then stopped them as they turned to leave him.

"Oh, I nearly forgot," he said. "Councillor Hibbert and the anonymous letter. I'm afraid it's been stamped on by very high authority. The word has come down that it is not to be investigated."

"Any reason given?"

"No. The level of authority is such that it does not have to give reasons. And nobody argues. I still think there might be something in it but I've got enough hassle at the moment without sticking my neck out.

"And of course," he added, "the Latimer Mercy theft is in no way connected with the investigation into the disappearance of Miss Porter." He gave them a look of exaggerated innocence. "Very proud of his collection, Councillor Hibbert. Always happy to show it to people, I'm told."

Maltravers stared at him. "You're a bloody funny copper," he said.

Jackson returned his stare reproachfully. "Can't think what you mean. You brought the letter to us and I'm just informing you of the official position. I think you're entitled to know that. Well, if you'll forgive me I've got a lot to do. Give my compliments to the Dean. Goodnight."

The Dean's wife opened the door to Maltravers, Tess and Melissa, her formidable presence softened by shock and sympathy.

"How kind of you to come," she said as they entered the hall. "We have both been most concerned for you. Please come through."

They went into the room at the rear of the house where the

French windows gave on to the evening garden. The Dean rose as they walked in, kissed Melissa and Tess and shook Maltravers' hand with both of his and held it for a long moment.

"I wish I could find words of comfort," he said. "We are so dreadfully, dreadfully sorry."

"We're very sorry about what happened this morning. In the post."

The Dean let go of his hand and made a gesture of dismissal.

"It was dreadful, of course, but I am much more concerned for Miss Porter. And for yourselves. Please. Sit down. A sherry, perhaps?"

When the drinks had been distributed, the Dean clearly wished to talk about what had been going through his mind during the day.

"I cannot understand the actions of this man," he began. "I have worked from the assumption that he must be in some way mad, but even madness must have some manner of insane logic. Whatever his reasons for abducting Miss Porter, what are his motives for what has happened since? The terrible business of the hand on the door may have been some sort of perverted action against you and Miss Davy, who are Miss Porter's friends. But I have no connection with Miss Porter at all except for our very brief meetings at the weekend. I've been racking my brains to try and find some sort of connection which would link everything together. Perhaps if that can be found it would assist, although quite frankly, I cannot see how. And of course any speculation is meaningless when the most urgent matter is to find Miss Porter. I understand the police are still not treating this matter as a murder inquiry? I'm sorry, that was not a tactful question."

"That's all right, Dean," said Maltravers. "It's something that we are having to face. There are no reports that she has been treated for her injuries."

As regret and sympathy flowed from the Dean's silent response to his remark, Maltravers reflected on what he had been saying. Now that the Dean had been directly involved there appeared no sense whatever in what was happening. And if Powell were not caught, would it stop with the Dean? Maltravers

106

shook his mind loose of that dark and threatening alley of his thoughts in which lay all manner of possible evil.

They stayed for an hour of shared condolence and concern, Maltravers' mind constantly returning to the contrasting image of the hard neon light, steel desks and ordered efficiency of the police station where the matter which encompassed them in strained and painful politeness was the focal point of ringing telephones, accumulating paperwork and dispassionate routine. The two perceptions of the same reality were irreconcilable.

"I still have no adequate words of comfort," the Dean said as they rose to leave. "And I do not think there are any. That's not the sort of confession senior clergymen should make I'm afraid, but in these circumstances I feel that anything I try to say might sound patronising and hollow. All I can say is that Miss Porter is constantly in our prayers."

They thanked their hosts and left, affected by their distress and compassion. As they turned out of the gate from the Dean's, they heard the chink of glass from the house next door and saw Webster on the front step with two milk bottles in his hand. They waited as he walked down the short path to them.

"I'm glad I've seen you," he said. "I know about what happened this morning of course and want to express my sympathy. I thought you might like to know that I hold a weekly prayer meeting in my house and tonight we said prayers for Miss Porter. Miss Targett was with us and I think it helped to comfort her."

"Oh, yes, Miss Targett," said Tess. "Thank you for what you did in the Chapter House the other evening. I'm afraid there was nothing we could find to say to her."

Webster smiled. "There is nothing, however dreadful, that cannot be eased by knowledge of the love of God. I am sure the Dean must have told you that."

"Not in so many words," said Maltravers. "But we are very grateful for all the help people are giving us at the moment."

"Is there any news about this man the police are looking for?" Webster asked. He suddenly became aware that he was still holding the milk bottles and looked uncertain what to do with them.

"Certainly not up to earlier this evening."

"Well, the evildoer will be punished," Webster said quietly. "The Lord will find his instrument."

Maltravers wondered how the self-sufficient Madden would feel at being the handservant of the Almighty, whom he probably regarded as a sort of elevated Chief Constable who should let His agents carry out the duties of retribution after He'd laid down the broad general policy.

"I wanted to give you something," Webster went on. "It may be of some help. If you have a moment . . . ?"

They followed him into the house, a narrow, disproportionately high building sandwiched between the Dean's and another equally imposing structure in the terrace. The small front room was sparsely furnished with an old-fashioned bookcase against one wall. Webster went to one shelf and realised he was still carrying the bottles. He put them down and pulled down a brown leather-bound volume and handed it to Maltravers. It was a copy of the Vercaster Mystery Plays.

"You may know they were written by the monk Stephen of Vercaster," he said. "The current productions are only an adaptation but the originals are of real merit. They were written to be performed by ordinary people and to remind them that our everyday lives and what we do in them cannot be separated from God's purpose and the path that Christ showed us." He looked at Maltravers earnestly. "There are meanings and there are reasons for everything that happens in the pattern that God has ordained. I take great comfort from that and from trying to follow God's intentions even though they are a great mystery. I think you might find it of help to dwell on those thoughts."

"Thank you," said Maltravers, slightly uncomfortable in the face of such sincerity. "I'll read them with interest."

"It really is very kind of you, Matthew," Melissa said tactfully. "But if you'll forgive us we must be getting back. I'm expecting a telephone call from Canon Cowan."

They said goodnight and continued their short walk back to Punt Yard.

"I'm sorry about that," Melissa said. "Matthew always means well but you didn't need all that at the moment."

"Odd, isn't it?" said Maltravers. "The Dean never mentioned God once but I got much more from him than from our young friend's religious overkill. And I'm afraid I've got too many black thoughts about Diana to accept his assurances of God's purpose behind all this. He can have his convictions. I just want Powell found . . . and ten minutes alone in a locked room with him."

"Come on, stop that," said Tess. "Those are bad-vibe thoughts and won't do anything to help Diana. Revenge won't do any of us any good."

"I'm not in the mood for liberal humanism at the moment. Don't worry, I expect I'll get back to it."

Chapter 10

REPORTED SIGHTINGS OF Arthur Powell — all of them erroneous when checked — were reaching the Vercaster incident room at an average of four an hour but Madden accepted them with no sense of frustration. They represented a methodical process of police co-operation from which escape was unthinkable. Every force in Britain would respond to a Madden-inspired request for assistance as long as the hunt for Powell and Diana Porter continued. It was a period between the crime and the inevitable arrest which brought its own satisfactions. Inquiries had shown that Powell's passport had expired two years previously and had not been renewed, so he was somewhere in Britain, where millions of people had been made familiar with his face. Even though Diana's hand had been sent from London two days earlier, Madden unswervingly authorised checks on sightings in the remotest spots; explanations could be sorted out later when Powell was arrested and in the meantime textbook procedures would be followed.

As Madden read the reports from as far apart as Grasmere and Birmingham, Brighton and York, a teleprinter message was being received in Scotland Yard from Los Angeles and was immediately transmitted to Vercaster where Jackson watched it spell itself out. When it was complete, he took it from the machine and read it through again. There had been a break in the filming of the television series in which Peter Sinclair was appearing, following an accident to one of the leading members of the cast. For several days he had not been required and had flown back to Britain. He was now back in America and the Los Angeles police wanted to know if they should question him further. Jackson took the message through to Madden.

"Returned to Heathrow early on Saturday morning, flew back

110

Wednesday evening our time," he said. "You say this was an unexpected interruption?"

"That's how I understand it, sir. He would not have anticipated the opportunity."

"So that means he suddenly decided, faced with the completely unexpected, to return to England, murder a woman he hadn't seen for a year, nail one hand to a door then post the other to the Dean on his way to the airport. We have no reported sightings of him in Vercaster where Maltravers at least would have recognised him. Doesn't look very promising, sergeant."

"No, sir. What reply shall I give Los Angeles?"

Madden pondered for a few moments. "Request that they interview him again," he said finally. "He must know what has happened if he was here. Let's see what his story is about why he came back and what he did. But I don't think we need concern ourselves unduly with this, sergeant."

"No, sir. Thank you, sir." After the previous day's experience following Maltravers' visit to Belsthwaite, Jackson was keeping his behavioural nose scrupulously clean. He returned to the incident room and arranged for Madden's request to be sent to Los Angeles, then started helping with the endless mountain of paperwork. The investigation had reached a curious stage where Vercaster was the one place virtually nothing was happening; they were currently the receiving post for the scattered information coming in, waiting for that brief moment of elation in the midst of the repetitive tedium when someone, somewhere, found and arrested Arthur Powell.

Full of misgivings about the wisdom, legality and possible success of the venture, Tess was discussing their proposed visit to Hibbert with Maltravers. Following Jackson's broad hint, he was determined to do it. His suggestion, which he readily admitted was half-baked and riddled with faults, was that they should simply turn up at Hibbert's house, introduce themselves, evince an interest in ancient books, rely on Hibbert's reported willingness to show off his collection and have Tess somehow lure him out of the room while Maltravers tried to get into the locked cupboard.

"Don't examine it too closely," he said. "It won't stand careful scrutiny."

"But even if we manage to do all that, he probably keeps the key on him," objected Tess. It was the latest of many irrefutable objections which Maltravers had brushed aside.

"But perhaps there's a spare somewhere. The point is we don't lose anything by trying. Even if there's no connection with Diana, it could sort out the theft business. If I can get into the cupboard and the Latimer Mercy is there I can tell Jackson and the police will have to do something then. Look, suppose . . . just suppose . . . there is a connection with Diana. You surely don't want to risk missing an opportunity of helping to find her?" He let the question hang in the air and Tess had no answer.

Hibbert lived in a large 1930s house set in its own grounds on the northern borders of Vercaster. When they arrived he was at home, his business activities now consisting largely of regular negotiations with his accountants to avoid the worst excesses of the tax system while his two sons took care of day-to-day matters. Maltravers apologised for calling unannounced and introduced Tess and himself.

"We've been told about your book collection," he said and noted the instant spasm of pride and condescension that flickered across Hibbert's florid face. "If it's not inconvenient, we would greatly like to see it. We can come back another time if you wish, of course."

"Not at all, not at all." Hibbert spoke as though addressing a visitation of humble and suitably obsequious ratepayers. "I was only reading through the Finance Committee minutes, but they can wait. Come in."

Having indicated that, while all his leisure moments were occupied by turning his benevolent mind to the interests of Vercaster and its citizens, a sense of attentive courtesy was still the hallmark of his behaviour, Hibbert led them through to his library. It was a staggering treasure house of fine leather and the printed word.

From floor to ceiling, virtually all round the walls, were ranked the rows of books. The sheer number of them, their spines in varying shades of golden brown, plum, stark black, rich green, all

112

glinting with gold tooling, was remarkable in a private house. The south-facing room with its wide bow window was light and elegant, its furniture consisting only of a large polished table with a reading lamp in the centre, mahogany leather wing-chairs, a small bureau in the window alcove and the corner cupboard to which their eyes instantly flew. It was of polished oak with a curved front and a decorated brass keyhole and looked, quite illogically, locked.

"I don't know what your particular interests are," said Hibbert, "but let me show you this first of all."

This was an edition of Holinshed's *Chronicles*, an impressive start by any standards, and was followed by a clearly regularly displayed selection including Foxe's *Booke of Martyrs*, rare editions of Virgil, Homer and Horace, an original edition of Byron's *Childe Harold*, signed first editions of the Waverley novels and *Johnson's Dictionary*. Maltravers observed that the offerings did not include the esoteric or obscure; Hibbert's pleasure was not to boast to specialists but to reasonably educated people. His visitors made suitably appreciative noises indicating that the mere possession of such works enhanced their host's reputation, while seeking an excuse for the diversion they needed. Tess finally found it with a work by Repton on landscape gardening.

"I was admiring your garden when we arrived," she said ingenuously. "Is it as superb at the back of the house?"

"My dear, it is unique," Hibbert replied pompously. "It contains every flower or plant mentioned by Shakespeare. As an actress, I'm sure . . . ?"

"How wonderful!" Maltravers controlled his features as Tess went spectacularly over the top. "Every one? *Could* I see it?" She had touched correctly, if by chance, on another of Hibbert's sources of self-importance. "It must be remarkable."

Hibbert's gesture of self-deprecation only served to magnify his conceit. "Of course. It will be my pleasure. Mr Maltravers?"

Maltravers suddenly took a great interest in a set of bound copies of the Spectator, admitted a quite true ignorance of or interest in gardens and asked if he might be allowed to browse instead.

"Examine anything you wish," insisted Hibbert. "Miss Davy, if you would come this way."

Tess gave Maltravers an idiotic grimace behind the councillor's back and they left the room. Maltravers listened to Hibbert's voice receding down the hall and then stepped swiftly to the cupboard, grasped the handle and pulled. It was locked, but the temptation to see how kind the fates were being was irresistible. He glanced round the room for a place where the key might be kept.

The central table had a single drawer but it contained only a few sheets of paper and a magnifying glass. The only other immediate possibility was the bureau in the window. It was unlocked. It was also depressingly tidy — Maltravers held that excessive tidiness was the sign of a sick mind — and only a few moments showed there was no key of any sort in it. The two drawers below held nothing more than a collection of book catalogues and writing paper. Maltravers closed the lower drawer and stood up, staring at the bureau for a moment before turning to look round the room again as a distant bell of re-collection sounded in his brain. He frowned as his eyes searched for any other possible hiding place, then he whirled round to stare at the top of the bureau again. Across the top was carved a row of small wooden knobs, each about half an inch high; towards the right hand end one was significantly lower than the rest. Maltravers was mentally thrown back to his childhood, to the home of a long-dead uncle and a regular delight for Melissa and himself when they visited him. He pulled the bureau open again and stretched his hand to depress the irregular knob which had been worn down with use. With the slight click of a hidden spring, a small panel fell open on invisible hinges.

"God bless you, Uncle Donald, wherever you are," he breathed.

He reached inside the secret compartment behind the panel and pulled out a small key. For a second he gazed at it in amazement, then crossed the room and pushed it into the lock of the corner cupboard. It was the right key.

The cupboard contained about thirty volumes but an immediate glance showed there was nothing as big as the Latimer Mercy.

He stretched his fingers to feel behind them but there was nothing hidden. Deflated with disappointment, he glared angrily at the shelves for a moment, then one title caught his eye. He pulled down the volume and flicked through it hastily then returned it and took another at random as a smile of surprise filled his face. He took out half a dozen other volumes and looked at them rapidly, pausing occasionally when he came to an illustration.

"Well, well, well," he muttered to himself. Suddenly he became aware that time was passing, returned all the books to their places, relocked the cupboard and put the key back in its hiding place. As Tess, laughing unnecessarily loudly, as a warning, returned with Hibbert, he was apparently engrossed in one of Addison's essays.

"Miss Davy was saying that you have a luncheon appointment," said Hibbert and Maltravers rightly concluded that some excuse for retreat had become desirable. "But if you would care to call again . . . ?"

"That's most kind," Maltravers told him. "We're very grateful for your hospitality but we must be off. I think I'd have to go to a stately home to see anything to rival this." His waving arm embraced the library and Hibbert almost visibly swelled even more.

"I don't wish to be immodest, but I think you're right," he said. He was a man who would suffer from immodesty in nothing.

"Who started the collection?" Maltravers asked as they prepared to go.

"My grandfather, Alderman Horatio Hibbert, began it in a small way but it was my father who really established it. I've added where I can but it was virtually complete at the time of father's death."

"Of course, your family's been in Vercaster for some time." To Tess's mystification Maltravers appeared to have a sudden interest in the subject.

"Since 1855 when the family business was established. We were originally Suffolk yeomen and my grandfather came here determined to make his fortune." Hibbert smiled graciously. "I think we can say he succeeded. Mind you, our motto has always

115

been service to the community. Grandfather was elected to the council in 1884 and there has been a Hibbert on the council virtually ever since."

"Remarkable," said Maltravers, demonstrating a correct level of awe. "I think I saw your grandfather's tomb in the cathedral. A most impressive list of achievements."

"A family tradition," Hibbert maintained stoutly. "Our policy has been integrity in business, service to the community and morality in conduct. Sounds a bit old-fashioned today perhaps but I personally mourn the loss of the decency which my grandfather epitomised." Maltravers noticed the look of glazed disbelief spread across Tess's face but made one final remark.

"Very different today I fear." It was a sure touch and brought the response he expected.

"My grandfather would have been appalled with what has happened, Mr Maltravers!" Hibbert was close to actually shouting. "I tell you, this city and this nation would be infinitely better if it followed his standards. My father maintained them and so do I, but the licentiousness of behaviour today is undermining the very fabric of the society we have built up. If I had my way in such matters, I . . ."

"Good heavens, is that really the time?" Maltravers interrupted before Hibbert could reach the full force of his flow of righteous indignation. "Please excuse us, but we do have that lunch appointment."

As they were leaving, Maltravers remarked on the portraits in the hall, obviously of the two previous generations of upright Hibberts, the Alderman bearded and patrician, his son smooth, confident and correct, robed as Mayor.

"Great men," Hibbert said simply. "Of unblemished reputation and faultless behaviour." He smiled with family pride. "They were Hibberts." The surname was pronounced adjectivally, incorporating all manner of virtues, and his visitors looked at them again with suitably polite regard before they left.

"Well?" demanded Tess as she slammed the car door.

"Just a moment. Wave to Councillor Hibbert, he likes to be waved at."

Tess turned and gave Hibbert a dazzling smile as he stood

self-importantly on his own doorstep and Maltravers turned the car on the gravel drive.

"Did you find the key?" she said through smile-gritted teeth.

"Oh, yes, I found the key." Tess turned to him, her entire face a question. "And I looked in the cupboard. But I didn't find the Latimer Mercy."

Tess's face flopped with disappointment. "We went through all that to find nothing."

"I wouldn't say that. I did find what is in that cupboard and why he keeps it locked. It contains what polite people call erotica but may be bluntly termed upmarket hard porn with very specific illustrations." He smiled in vulgar recollection. "Councillor Hibbert may not be our thief, but he is a dirty old man. And it appears to run in the family."

Chapter 11

IN THE EARLY hours of Saturday morning Maltravers and Tess were woken by a crash of thunder like an oak tree falling on a slate roof as a summer storm, boiled by the long spell of hot weather, erupted over Vercaster. They went to the bedroom window and looked out at the panorama of tumbling, muscular black clouds seething beyond the grey pinnacle of Talbot's Tower. Sheets of lightning spasmodically lit tower and cathedral with blinks of ice-coloured glare as the rattle of rain thrashed the two ancient Cedars of Lebanon that stood by the Lady Chapel. Dawn had long broken but the June sun was invisible, burning impassively somewhere above the turbulent breakers of cloud rolling back and forth across the city. Another clattering explosion right above the house made them jump and in the comparative silence that followed they heard Michael and Melissa's voices, then the click of a bedroom door and footsteps crossing the landing and descending the stairs.

"I'll go back to my room," Tess said. "Just for appearance's sake."

Maltravers remained at the window, watching bubbling rivulets race along the rain-lacquered pavements of Punt Yard from the engorged drains and thought about Diana, still possibly alive, somewhere out in the storm, helpless, mutilated and in endless pain. His face, which had smiled blandly at Hibbert the previous day, was layered with foreboding. It would be a long time before he really found his laughter again.

The storm moved away to the east, the thunderclaps now faint echoes of the earlier clamour, the rain easing, then ceasing. A sword of sunlight pierced the clouds and moved with surprising swiftness across the landscape of fast-dripping trees, drenched grass and battered flowers. Maltravers opened the window and listened to the gurgling drains and birdsong as the rising heat began to draw a ghostly steam from the ground. Distantly, a racing train gave a sweeping whistle and below him a milk-float jangled onto the cobbles of the yard.

"Morning!" the milkman shouted as he spotted Maltravers at the window. "Needed that. It's cleared the air." Maltravers smiled back at him but said nothing.

Joe Goldman called after breakfast, his unnatural sombreness, in total contrast to his usual bullying ebullience, another shadow in the aura of gathering gloom. Recordings by Diana of a cassette of children's stories had been cancelled, another actress had been found for a play at Manchester's Royal Exchange theatre, Joe's office was filled with messages of concern and condolence, including one from Zabinski.

"Still no news then?" Goldman asked.

"No."

"Do you think she's still alive, Gus?"

"I don't know what to think now. Every possibility is terrible."

"You won't believe this, Gus, but yesterday I went to the synagogue. Me in the synagogue? I asked for Rabbi Greenberg but he died twenty years ago. But I prayed for her, Gus."

"Thanks, Joe. I'll keep in touch." Maltravers recalled Jackson's remarks about the devastating effects of sudden death and how people had to cope in any way they could. In any other circumstances the thought of Joe Goldman by the Eastern wall would have been ludicrous; the fact that he had actually done it added another subtle shade of darkness to the agony of unknowing.

The police that morning knew a little more, but not about the elusive Arthur Powell; a report had arrived on the police interrogation of Peter Sinclair in California.

"He came back just for the sake of spending a few days in England, apparently," Jackson told Madden. "He cleared it with the studios and was quite open about it. Obviously he read about Miss Porter's disappearance while he was here but says she was just an old girlfriend he hadn't seen for a long time. His movements while he was here seem a bit vague. He stayed in his own flat in Islington, casually met acquaintances and went to see a couple of West End shows but in both cases he was alone. As far as I can make out, it's possible he came to Vercaster—but he completely denies doing so."

Madden held out his hand for the message from Los Angeles, then read it through for himself.

"There's no sense to it," he said as he finished. "I take it he's safe in Los Angeles for the time being."

"Apparently. The studios are catching up on lost time after the interruption and say it will be several weeks before anyone gets a break now."

"I take it he denies being the father of the child?"

"Absolutely. I rang Los Angeles to check that. He says it's at least ten months since he saw Miss Porter."

"All right. We'll leave him there for the time being but see if you can find any evidence that he has seen her since. The agent in London might know something. Or Maltravers. I still don't see this one, sergeant, but until Powell is found we'd better keep an eye on it."

Sinclair was an irritant to Madden, a bell ringing out of key that he could not fully silence, a flaw in the pattern that led neatly and logically to Arthur Powell, an irregularity that offended his sense of certainty. But he had no option but to turn some attention to it. Jackson started his inquiries with a visit to Punt Yard where he told Maltravers and Tess of the development.

"I can't help you on whether or not he's seen Diana since the affair," Maltravers said. "In fact I didn't even know about that until Joe Goldman told me. Acting's one of those professions where you might not see even very good friends for long periods. I'd seen a fair bit of her in recent weeks when we were working on her show for Vercaster but there are immense gaps when we were both doing other things. Tess, do you know anything?"

She shook her head. "I've been tied up for months. In fact, this is the first break I've had for nearly a year." She laughed briefly and without humour. "Not the sort of holiday I'd planned."

"I can give you some names and addresses of people who might be able to help," added Maltravers. "And you can try Joe, but as an agent he doesn't necessarily take much interest in his clients' private lives unless they start getting in the way of the job." He produced his diary and Jackson noted the names he read out.

"Oh, and I'm afraid we've been playing at detectives again," Maltravers said when they had finished. "We went to see Councillor Hibbert."

"Obviously I must officially disapprove," Jackson said straight-faced. "But as long as you lay before me any information which might assist the police, I don't think there'll be any trouble."

He listened with a widening smile to the extraordinary account of the visit.

"I don't think I can see an offence," he said at last. "You didn't break in, you didn't steal anything, and I can't charge you with bad manners. As for Councillor Hibbert . . . well there's no law against such a collection I expect. We certainly wouldn't get a search warrant on the strength of what you've told me. But I'll bear it in mind if I have any dealings with the gentleman." He looked at them both closely. "And of course, you will not be telling anyone else about this."

"It will be our secret," said Maltravers. "It still leaves the Latimer Mercy mystery unsolved but I imagine the police are not particularly worried about that at the moment."

"Some part of the machinery is ticking it over but, as you know, officially it's being regarded as unconnected with Miss Porter."

"But is it?"

"There's absolutely no logical connection at all between the two."

"And can you find a logical connection in what's happened regarding Diana? The Dean was remarking on that the other evening."

"That's a fair point and personally I accept it," Jackson replied. "But for obvious reasons we can't do anything more than the bare minimum about the theft; we are totally occupied on a very serious crime. And I honestly cannot see that finding out who stole the Latimer Mercy will help us find Miss Porter." He stood up. "Thank you for your assistance. I'll see if any of these people can throw more light on Mr Sinclair."

After the dramatic interruption of the storm, summer had re-settled itself and after lunch Tess and Maltravers decided to walk round the extensive remains of the city's Roman walls. On their way Maltravers bought a large plastic ball for Rebecca and bounced it thoughtfully as they walked in silence. The wall petered out in Hibbert's Park — named in memory of the founding-father Alderman — where they sat beside the lake in the marbled light and shade of a cascading weeping willow. For two hours they had not mentioned Diana's name and then Tess broke the tension. "I think I've accepted that she's dead," she said, keeping her voice very calm. Maltravers remained silent for several minutes, spinning the ball between his hands and staring at it.

"Let's walk back by the cathedral," was all he finally said in reply.

The approach from the park was up the north-west-facing slope of the hill, giving the classic clear-angled view of the west end of the building which appeared on postcards in every tourists' shop in the town. They walked slowly up the long rise and paused on the broad path outside the door as the clock in Talbot's Tower sounded three ponderous strokes.

"It was just here that the Abbot of Vercaster defied Henry VIII's men during the Reformation," said Maltravers. "When he started calling down the vengeance of God on the king, they cut him down on the steps. At least that's the legend. There was a very heavy veil of Tudor propaganda drawn over it at the time." He looked thoughtfully at the great door with its rusty studs of nail heads. "Bloodshed has frequently stained the Church." He started idly bouncing the ball again as they continued to walk along the south side of the cathedral and back to Punt Yard. As they passed the flying buttresses of the tower, the ball struck a large flint and bounced behind him; he turned back and stooped to pick it up. As he did so there was a scream from a woman walking towards them with her husband, and a large piece of broken masonry crashed down and caught him on the hip. The glancing impact sent him sprawling across the gravel as Tess, alerted by the woman's scream, turned and cried his name. He sat up, grimacing with pain and the first thing his eyes focussed on was a painted sign warning passers-by to beware of falling masonry.

"It's all right, it hardly touched me," he said as Tess dropped down on her knees beside him. "Let me get up."

He rose gingerly to his feet, rubbing his thigh where a dark streak ran across his grey slacks, then staggered against Tess.

"I'm rapidly going off Vercaster," he said.

"You could have been killed!" she cried.

"But I wasn't."

"Come and sit down." Tess helped him to hobble towards a wrought-iron seat well away from the tower. The woman who had screamed ran up to them with her husband.

"I saw it falling!" she cried. "I couldn't do anything . . . I just screamed . . . Oh, God!" She seemed more shattered by the incident than Maltravers.

"Thank you, I'm all right," he assured her. "There's nothing broken."

"But it's appalling!" her husband broke in. "That damned tower's unsafe. They want scaffolding round it until it's properly repaired. Anybody could have . . ." His tirade was brought to a halt by the arrival of the Dean, moving at the closest he could manage to a run.

"Mr Maltravers!" he panted. "I was just leaving the Refectory and saw everything. Are you all right?"

"It's a miracle that he is." The man was back in full flow. "Look, I'm a civil engineer. I don't know who you are but you're obviously connected with the cathedral and I'm telling you the state of that tower is a disgrace. It's a menace to life and limb. If this gentleman wants a witness as to what happened, I'll gladly . . ."

In pain, surrounded by Tess's shock, the woman's hysteria, the man's bombast and the Dean's distress, Maltravers decided only he could calm things down.

"I am all right," he said firmly. "It's nothing worse than a bruise. I'm not holding anyone responsible. If you're a civil engineer, you'll know how difficult it is to maintain anything that ancient." He gestured towards Talbot's Tower. "We had one hell of a storm this morning and part of the fabric must have been loosened. There are warning notices up and I don't think you can do any more, Dean."

"Oh, you're the Dean are you?" The man exploded again and Maltravers realised he had only given him more ammunition.

"Well if you and your Chapter spent more time looking after this building instead of sending money to damned terrorists in Africa who call themselves freedom fighters, then . . ."

"He's not real," Maltravers muttered to Tess.

"Perhaps we can just go inside for a few minutes until Augustus recovers," she said firmly, taking Maltravers' arm. "Can you come with us please, Dean?" She gave the couple an extravagant smile. "Thank you *so* much. I think it's more important at the moment that my friend sits somewhere quiet for a little while."

Leaving the visitor with his continuing views of Third World aid unspoken, the three of them walked slowly into the cathedral.

"I cannot apologise too much," the Dean began. "As if enough has not happened already and now something like this . . ."

"Dean, it was an accident that could have happened to anyone. Please do not distress yourself. I think it will be better if I try and walk a bit and a cup of tea would be very welcome."

They walked together out of the cathedral and round the cloisters to the Refectory where the Dean, by now as agitated and concerned as a mother hen, made them sit at a table while he brought the tea, the cups rattling and spilling over as the tray trembled in his hands. Reaction was catching up with Maltravers and taking a greater toll than the increasing discomfort in his hip. As Tess suggested they should leave, the Dean suddenly sprang up and asked them to wait, then dashed off to return a few moments later carrying a walking stick.

"I've just borrowed this from Mr Marsh in the tourists' shop," he explained.

Limping awkwardly, Maltravers left with Tess, the Dean insisting on escorting them through the south transept door to Punt Yard. As they reached the house, Michael and Webster approached from the main road.

"What on earth's happened to you?" Michael asked.

"Talbot's Tower has been throwing things at me. Fortunately with a not very good aim."

Michael was clearly as appalled as the Dean but more immediately practical.

"We'll have to look into this," he said. "Odd flints are one thing but this sounds much more serious. Matthew, can you go and check and we'll find out exactly which section of the tower it's from and then have someone make a proper examination."

As Webster set off, they went into the house where Melissa, accustomed to taking childhood accidents in her stride, produced lint, cotton wool, sticking plaster and witch-hazel.

"Cold compress for a while," she instructed Tess. "Then make a pad of lint soaked in the witch-hazel and tape it over the bruise. You're sure it's nothing worse?"

"I'm not broken," Maltravers assured her.

By the time he and Tess came downstairs again, the Dean had left with the walking stick and Webster was back talking to Michael.

"It's from the old part of the tower below the extension," Michael explained. "It's the section that's caused us most problems. I'm afraid we've got a fair collection of bits and pieces which have fallen but Matthew says this is the biggest he has seen for some time. I can only add my apologies, Augustus."

"I imagine it was the storm that did it," he replied. "Act of God you might say."

Webster, who was hovering uncertainly, said he had to leave to assist with the preparations for the schools' concert in the cathedral that evening, panicked briefly when he could not find the spare violin strings he had been carrying earlier, and departed.

"I'd just been to buy them when I met Canon Cowan," he said as he left. "Somebody's always snaps just before the start. Will you be coming this evening?"

"I think Augustus had better stay home and rest," said Melissa. "But the rest of us will be there. We don't want anything to spoil it for the children."

Maltravers spent the remainder of the afternoon in increasing pain and rising irritation. By the time the others were preparing to leave he could only move his leg with difficulty.

"Take a couple of these," Melissa said, shaking two white tablets from a bottle into her cupped hand. "And just stay still and rest it. And you'd better not have a drink. These are fairly powerful. See you later unless you're in bed."

After they had gone, Maltravers idly picked up the bottle of analgesics, the label of which made no reference to alcohol. Conscientiously, he added extra tonic to his gin.

Television on a Saturday evening in June, he decided, was clearly part of a Government scheme to reduce the national consumption of electricity. He dozed off a few minutes into an artificially created seaside entertainment when drowsiness overcame the fascination of the spectacularly awful. The pain in his leg, returning as the effects of the tablets wore off, conjured dreams in his semi-conscious mind which vanished when he was abruptly woken by a car door slamming outside. He blinked for a few moments then cautiously changed his position in the chair, his face creasing with the shots of pain. He took two more tablets from the bottle and washed them down with the remains of his drink, then stared grumpily at the still chattering television, his mind trying to recapture what he had been dreaming. All he could remember was that it was something about Belsthwaite.

The dream was irrecoverable but his mind wandered back to their visit as he gazed without seeing at the television screen. Elusively dancing in his brain was the thought that they had learned or seen or been told something there that was important; after vainly pursuing it for a while, he let it drift away to be replaced with another gadfly impression that something else had occurred which was also significant. Uneasy sleep overtook him again, this time bringing a dream of Diana, shrieking pitifully like a wild animal in a snare as, his movements becoming slower and slower, he limped towards the sound. It became so terrible that his conscious mind threw him back to wakefulness with a shudder as the front door opened and he heard the voices of the others in the hall.

126

From the television screen a news announcer was saying that the hunt for Diana Porter was now being treated as a murder inquiry.

Chapter 12

"IT's VERY UNUSUAL when we have no body and we have been careful to say that we are only *treating* it as a murder inquiry, not that it is one." David Jackson looked round the impassive faces of his listeners the following morning. "I imagine you find that somewhat semantic but it does make a difference. The point is that there are no reports whatever of Miss Porter being given medical treatment for her injuries and without that the chances of her still being alive are very remote indeed. I'm sorry."

Maltravers shifted awkwardly in his chair as the pain in his leg narrowed and bit.

"But it is still possible," he insisted. "She may have been treated by someone you don't know about."

"Believe me, I would like to think you're right but I feel it's only proper that I should explain the official viewpoint quite clearly. We can say without doubt that she has not been in any established or regular hospital or seen by any reputable doctor. The chances of her being treated by some unauthorised medical practitioner are very slim. And we have no indication that Powell could render her assistance, even assuming he wanted to."

"If it is Powell," said Maltravers.

"He's still the principal suspect, in fact he's really the only one." Jackson paused uncertainly for a moment. "I'm afraid this is additional distress for you, but the police surgeon is unable to say definitely whether either hand was severed while she was still alive or shortly after death. What he is certain of is that without treatment she must by now have died." He made a slight gesture of sympathy. The last time Diana had been in that room she had been alive and laughing and playing with Rebecca and in the silence that surrounded them were echoes of that moment.

"I would like to say on behalf of us all, sergeant, that we greatly appreciate your coming here this morning to tell us this," said Michael. "It is very unpleasant for you as well. I think, however, that we would probably all prefer to cling on to what little hope may remain."

After Jackson had gone, Melissa left to drive down to Sussex and bring Rebecca back and Michael went out on cathedral business. The day had the timeless quality of an English Sunday with its images of empty streets, shuttered shops and stillness in places of activity. Deciding that cautious exercise would be better for his leg than sitting still, Maltravers, leaning on a stick borrowed from Michael, walked with Tess down to the Verta again. They instinctively turned the opposite way from the path that would lead them to the ruined church where they had been with Diana the previous week and walked down river to where the Verta spilled over a weir and the shouts of laughter from the gathered children mingled with the rushing sounds of cascading water. The normality of the scene was painfully alien to their mood.

In the afternoon they sat in the garden, Tess reading and Maltravers stretched on a sun lounger. Clouds of greenfly speckled the sunlit air and cushions of pinks near where they sat were heavy with the drone of bees. Maltravers idly watched a butterfly flicker near them until it finally settled on Tess's auburn hair and stayed there for several moments until she turned to look at him.

"How's your leg?" she asked.

"Much better." He stretched it experimentally and a spasm of pain crossed his face. "It's the waiting that's worse."

The sense of inertia was becoming intolerable. Maltravers had frequently imagined being faced with a crime that baffled the police and solving it with some brilliant flash of deduction; it was not an uncommon human fantasy. The reality, he now knew, was not like that. It was the police, not eccentric gifted amateurs, who investigated and solved murders. His total contribution so far had been a ridiculous and unprofitable journey to Belsthwaite, the net result of which had been a row with Madden. And yet, as he tried to see straight through his confusing emotional involvement, the insistent impression remained of knowing certain things which he was quite unable to recognise. The fanciful genius of his daydreams was turned to a sense of inadequacy and despair by what had actually happened. The garden gate opened and Rebecca trotted happily across the lawn to them, followed by Melissa.

"Nana brought this," said the little girl and thrust a glove puppet of an attractively stupid-looking duck at her uncle. Maltravers put it on his hand and accompanied his manipulations with quacking noises. Tess went into the house to make a cup of tea and Melissa took her place on the rug.

"I've been thinking while I was driving," she said. "Why was the hand actually put on our door? Obviously whoever did it was taking the risk of being seen when he could have sent it through the post as he did with the Dean. Who do you think it was meant for?"

"Possibly all of us," said Maltravers, making Rebecca giggle as he pinched her nose with the duck's beak.

"But suppose it was specifically one of us?"

"Tess and I knew her best, so we're the obvious targets."

"Yes, but just suppose it was Michael. There is a clear link between him and the Dean and the cathedral and if this man Powell has something against the Church it could make some sort of perverted sense. Do you know anything about that?"

"No. As he's Welsh, I assume he's probably a Methodist or one of the Nonconformist sects."

"The Primitive Methodists are very narrow minded," said Melissa.

"Maybe so, but we go back to your first point. Why didn't he send it to Michael through the post and avoid the risk of discovery?" Maltravers put the puppet on Rebecca's hand and watched her as she toddled away, clumsily working it. "It's as good a theory as any but until the police find Powell it's just another guess." He looked at his sister and smiled oddly. "The only thing that can be said about the hand on the door is that it removes suspicion from me."

"You?" Melissa had obviously never considered the possibility. "The police can't suspect you."

"Yes they can. David Jackson's never said it but it's a well-known fact that murderers almost invariably know their victims. They've obviously considered the possibility. However, equally obviously I couldn't have nailed the hand to the door. David Jackson himself is a witness to that."

Melissa was offended that such a thought had ever entered anyone's mind.

"I expect the same goes for me as well."

"For all of us. And for a number of other people. The Dean for example."

"Oh, Augustus, this is ridiculous! You can't be serious."

"I don't imagine we're high on the list of suspects. Powell's actions — particularly the fact that he hasn't come forward — make him the obvious line of investigation. But if it turns out not to be him . . . well, where do we go from there?"

"There's nobody else. Apart from this Sinclair person."

Maltravers shook his head. "I can't see it. And at the moment I don't think the police can either. It just seems a very odd coincidence that he came back."

First thing on Monday morning, Miss Craven, the Bishop's secretary, efficiently tackled the post, slitting open each envelope with a long slender paper-knife shaped like a sword. She stopped and thrust her fingers into one foolscap envelope and could feel nothing inside. Frowning, she turned it upside down, squeezed the sides slightly and shook it experimentally. A long lock of fair hair spilled onto the lime-green blotter on her desk, followed by a small piece of paper which fluttered to the floor. She picked it up and turned it over to read the typewritten message on the other side:

And ye, in any wise, keep yourselves from the accursed thing, lest ye make yourselves accursed.

As the daughter, granddaughter and niece of clergymen, Miss Craven prided herself on her knowledge of the Bible, but the quotation was not immediately familiar. She read it again then casually examined the lock of hair with a puzzled and slightly vexed expression. Anything other than the most correct and

131

regular of correspondence was almost unheard of at the Bishop's Palace. Finally she crossed the room and took a Concordance from the bookshelf in which she discovered that the passage was part of the eighteenth verse of the sixth chapter of Joshua, which settled the irritation in her mind. She carefully put the hair and its enigmatic message to one side and calmly continued with the rest of the mail, sorting it into piles of relative importance and urgency. All the envelopes were put together to have their stamps removed later to help raise funds for the Red Cross. Precisely as the clock on the mantelpiece chimed half past nine she picked up all the mail and walked through to the Bishop's study, knocking discreetly on the door before entering.

"Good morning, my Lord," she said. "Quite a deal of post today including a reply from the Archbishop. There's also one from Downing Street and a most charming letter of thanks from . . ." She stopped in mid-sentence as a look of horrified realisation filled her face. "Dear God!" She was staring at the hair and its note which she had kept separate from the rest of the post. As the Bishop looked at her with concern she dumbly held them out towards him.

"I think you had better call the police, Miss Craven," he said.

Monday morning's post was, fortunately, the lightest of the week for the Bishop and there were only twenty-two envelopes to sort out. Half of them bore some printed indication to connect them with their contents, three were handwritten and could be similarly identified and another three were in distinctive italic typewriter face. The remaining five were sent in separate polythene bags for examination in conjunction with the note itself. The note did not bear any fingerprints. As police were sent to Diana's flat again, this time to see if they could find any samples of her hair, consideration was given to the wording.

"Joshua," Madden said tersely, "fought the battle of Jericho of course."

"Yes, sir," said Jackson. "In fact the walls come tumbling down a couple of verses later." Madden looked at him in surprise. "There's a Bible in the station, sir. I looked it up."

"You amaze me," Madden said drily. "I trust there's not about to be a similar occurrence in this investigation. Anyway, what do you make of it?"

Jackson shrugged his shoulders. "Nothing really, sir. It's just another inexplicable . . ." He stopped abruptly as Madden's flattened hand slammed hard on the top of his desk.

"It is *not* inexplicable! Nothing is inexplicable. We are just not seeing the explanation." Madden pinched his nose so hard that red pressure marks remained when he let go. "I am beginning greatly to dislike this case. A diligent and methodical hunt has failed to discover the whereabouts of our chief suspect and I am being constantly faced with events which are regarded as unconnectable mysteries. There are links which we are failing to identify." He raised his hand and itemised points on his fingers. "One, Maltravers brings Miss Porter to Vercaster. Two, Powell is seen in Vercaster. Three, Miss Porter meets the Dean and the Bishop among others and then disappears as does Powell. Four, parts of her body reappear in Vercaster and now we may assume some of her hair has done so as well. Now, what can we possibly deduce from this latest incident?"

Jackson was beginning to feel a certain sympathy for Madden, whose considerable reputation had been built on a long series of textbook investigations which unfailingly followed the rules. He had once relentlessly caught a child-killer by fingerprinting the entire population of a village. But this case required imagination and a flair for the bizarre in which patient, professional police routine was not producing results.

"On the basis that it is Miss Porter's hair," he began cautiously, thinking as he proceeded, "it seems to follow that she is the accursed thing. The Bishop would appear to be being warned to have nothing to do with her."

"He can't have anything to do with her if she's dead."

"There have been prayers said for her safety in the cathedral. Admittedly not by the Bishop but he's obviously connected with them."

There was a knock on Madden's office door and another detective sergeant came in.

"We've had a report from the lab, sir. They've identified the

133

envelope. It was posted second class in Islington on Friday afternoon."

"Thank you, sergeant," said Madden. "Fingerprints?"

"Being done now, sir."

"Right," said Madden as the door closed behind him. "Is that where Powell is hiding? With a little elementary disguise it could serve as well as anywhere."

"Sinclair's flat is in Islington, sir." Jackson reminded him.

"Sinclair?" For a moment Madden looked blank. "Oh, our friend in America. But he went back . . . when was it? . . . Wednesday. This thing to the Bishop was posted on Friday."

"Accomplice possibly. Perhaps an unwitting one who just agreed to post a letter for him? Sergeant Neale's still checking his story but as far as I understand there's nothing so far to positively exclude him as a suspect."

Madden remained silent for a moment then pressed a switch on the intercom on his desk and asked for Inspector Barratt to come in. By the time the Inspector had joined them, he had marshalled his thoughts.

"I want all those principally concerned to be interviewed again," he said. "See if they can remember anything else. I want Neale's report on Sinclair's movements while in Britain as soon as possible and a full report on fingerprints on that envelope. I take it we have the secretary's and the postman's. And check anything you find connecting it to the Islington sorting office with anything found on the package sent to the Dean. Even without the postmark that may confirm it also came from there. That will be all."

After they returned to the incident room, Inspector Barratt told Jackson to return to Punt Yard to talk to Maltravers and the others again.

"I'm afraid this investigation is proving somewhat irregular," said Jackson, as he turned to go. "It's not to Mr Madden's liking."

"No it's not, sergeant. And he doesn't like having me in charge of this room either. Mr Madden just does not like senior women police officers but I was the only one available when this thing began. However," she looked up at him from her desk, "Mr Madden likes lack of results even less so we'd all better get on with it."

Patiently Maltravers and the rest went over their statements again, desperately trying to remember details of inconsequential conversations and casual events, small incidents and gestures, but nothing seemed to emerge.

"When will you know if it's definitely Diana's hair?" Maltravers asked.

"When we find something in her flat," said Jackson. "The chances are there'll be something on her pillow or somewhere."

"And there's a possible link with Sinclair?"

"It may just be a coincidence that he happens to have a flat in Islington but in our business coincidences are not just shrugged off. Until something removes him definitely from the picture we're keeping an eye on him. At the moment, things keep happening to push him further into our line of vision."

Maltravers gently changed his position to relieve the ache that was starting to creep down his leg. Jackson noticed the movement.

"What's happened to you?"

"Oh, just a fleeting contact with a collapsing cathedral. It's much better today." He was interrupted by the phone ringing next to him. He picked it up, listened for a moment then said, "Yes, he's here. Hang on." He proferred the receiver to Jackson. "It's for you. Inspector Barratt."

Jackson listened for several seconds then said, "Good God, where the hell have they been?" He listened again, then asked for an address which he wrote in his notebook.

"All right," he said, "I'll be there in a few minutes." He rang off.

"Where the hell have who been?" asked Maltravers.

"The couple that Powell stayed with in Vercaster a week ago on Saturday. They've just rung the station."

"*What?* Why haven't they been in touch before?"

"Been on holiday apparently. We all assumed that Powell probably camped somewhere when he was down here, particularly when nobody said he had stayed with them. We checked the

135

hotels and boarding houses but there are dozens of places in Vercaster that do bed and breakfast unofficially during the tourist season." He consulted his notebook. "Do you know Acacia Street? It doesn't matter, I've got a map in the car. Stay where you are, I'll let myself out."

Acacia Street reminded Jackson of Sebastopol Terrace except that the houses had the added benefit of small front gardens. It was exactly the sort of drab, anonymous area that would appeal to Powell. As he unlatched the gate of number nineteen the curtain shifted slightly at the window and the front door was opened as he approached it.

"Mrs Dunn? Sergeant Jackson, Vercaster CID."

"Come in please. Here in the front room." He followed the sun-tanned woman with the excessively precise hair-style through to the room where the first thing that caught his eye was an enormous imitation sombrero hooked over the back of a dining-chair.

"I understand that Mr Arthur Powell stayed here a week ago Saturday," he said formally.

"Yes, he did. Here, sit yourself down. My husband's just upstairs but he'll be down in a minute. I didn't know what to think when I saw it in the paper. I mean, the man's a murderer isn't he?" Mrs Dunn seemed concerned that her own reputation would suffer from having had such a person beneath her roof.

"We just want him for questioning at the moment. I think it will be best if we start at the beginning. When did he arrive?"

Mrs Dunn settled and composed herself. Her narrative was refreshingly succinct.

"He arrived on the Saturday lunchtime — about half past twelve," she said. "At first I said we couldn't put him up because we were going away the next morning but he said it would only be for the one night and . . . well, he was such a pleasant person so I agreed. He was hardly in the house. He went out in the afternoon to look round the cathedral. I said he could watch television with us in the evening but he said he was going to a performance at the

Chapter House. He assured me he would not be late and I said it would be all right as long as it was before eleven. And on Sunday morning he left."

"And you knew nothing about what happened afterwards?"

"Not a thing. We flew to Benidorm on the Sunday lunchtime and only got back last night. It was only when I managed to have a look at the *Times* this morning that I saw his face. So of course I rang your people at once."

Jackson was thrown for a moment by the newspaper reference then realised she was talking about the *Vercaster Times*; it had not struck him as the sort of household in which the better known variety would be found.

"Did you have any conversation with him?"

"Very little. He was very polite and quiet — just the sort of person we prefer. But we really had hardly any time to talk."

From upstairs there came the sound of a lavatory being flushed, followed by the sound of someone descending. Then Mr Dunn, a neat and compact little man, entered the room. His wife introduced Jackson.

"I was just asking if your guest might have said anything that could assist us," Jackson said.

"I've just been thinking about that," Dunn replied and Jackson kept his face impassive as the image Dunn's remark created sprang into his mind. "He asked for directions."

"Directions? Where to? When?"

"When he was leaving. I saw him off and wished him a good journey. He asked which was the best road that would lead him towards Wales."

"Wales." Jackson smiled gratefully at Dunn. "That's a very useful piece of information, sir. Very useful indeed."

"No it's not. Not now." Dunn smiled knowingly. "You see I asked him if that's where he was going and he said just for a few days then he was moving on. And this was just over a week ago. So he won't be there now." Having neatly demolished the possibility he had set up, Dunn smiled cheerfully at Jackson and sat down in an armchair by the fireplace.

"It could still assist us," said Jackson. "If we can find where he was in Wales we may be able to trace him from there. I just want to radio this information into the police station then I'd like to see the room he used please."

Mrs Dunn was waiting in the hall when Jackson returned from the car.

"It's exactly as he left it," she said as they went up the stairs. "I glanced in on the Sunday morning after he'd gone and it was perfectly tidy so I decided to leave it until we came back. Of course I haven't been in it since I read the papers."

The Dunns did not take excessive trouble over their accommodation for visitors. The room was long overdue for decorating and the furniture was at best shabby. Jackson remarked that the bed had been made.

"He must have done that," said Mrs Dunn. "Very considerate."

"Did he have any luggage?"

"Just a few things in his side-car. He only brought his pyjamas and a towel in. I think his tent was in there as well."

Leaving room, perhaps, for a body, Jackson reflected.

"Can this room be locked?"

"Oh, yes. We always give guests the key then there can be no misunderstandings. You know what I mean."

"I must ask you to lock it as we leave and nobody must come in here until my colleagues arrive from the police station. They should be here fairly soon. In the meantime, I'll need formal statements from you and your husband."

As they turned to leave, Jackson glanced swiftly round the room. There was no evidence at all that anybody had ever stayed in it. The anonymous Powell had passed through and, typically, had left no trace of his personality behind.

The Dunns' statements added nothing to what they had already told him. Powell had left first thing after breakfast on the Sunday morning and Dunn assumed he had set straight off for Wales.

"He said nothing about staying in Vercaster for part of the day?" Jackson asked.

"Not a thing. It's a fair journey and I suppose he'd want to get going as soon as possible."

138

As Jackson was completing the statements, Higson and other officers arrived to start their investigation of the bedroom. Dunn, who appeared to have something on his mind, followed Jackson to the front gate.

"I think we've behaved quite properly in reporting this as soon as we could," he said.

"Indeed. We're very grateful." Jackson could feel some motive behind the remark.

"It's just that we do return our income tax forms to the Inland Revenue's satisfaction." Dunn gave a significant wink. "I'm sure you understand, sergeant."

Jackson realised that the fact he might have had a murderer in his house for whom there was a nationwide search following a particularly hideous crime was less important to Dunn than the money he obviously denied the income tax man.

"I'm investigating a murder, sir," he replied. "I've no interest in anything else."

The lock of hair and the note posted in Islington also brought fresh evidence. To nobody's surprise, it was Diana's hair, and one set of fingerprints on the envelope, belonging to someone in the Islington sorting office, was also found on the package containing Diana's hand which had been sent to the Dean. Saliva tests further showed that both items had been sent by the same person. But there were no available saliva samples from Powell to clinch the matter. The police felt they had taken a significant step forward but until the final pieces fell into place the picture was still maddeningly unclear.

Monday evening saw the second performance of the Mystery Plays, this time in the Vercaster Players' own theatre. For Maltravers it was at least another diversion to occupy his mind with something else. The plays went from the Nativity — engagingly performed by a cast of children — through to the Temptation of Christ in the Wilderness. The Shepherds' Play was a delight, with an hilarious scene in which they became increasingly drunk, pulling an endless collection of ingeniously contrived long-lost local delicacies from their sacks until the stage was littered with scattered offal. The contrast with their wonder and adoration as the angels appeared was effective and moving.

But once again it was Jeremy Knowles's Devil who dominated everything, wielding a bloody and vicious sword through the Slaughter of the Innocents, attending the Wedding at Cana as a sly and malevolent guest, peering resentfully round the side of the cave from which the resurrected Lazarus emerged. Christ's steadfast rejection of his seductive worldly inducements was no more than a temporary setback in his progress towards eventual triumph. He spat his parting words like venom:

> "Long in patience, I shall wait
> Till we meet at Hell's dark gate.
> Flamed and awful, red with blood,
> Evil then shall master Good . . ."

He stopped with his voice on a rising, uncompleted note, then strode unnecessarily across the stage, losing the sense of direct conflict with Christ.

"He's forgotten his lines," Maltravers murmured sympathetically to Tess.

"Death triumphant . . ." a voice said from the wings and Knowles appeared to recover himself.

"Death triumphant . . ." he began but it was obviously not enough. Before the prompter could come in again he was riskily ad libbing.

"Death triumphant loud shall sing." There was the fraction of a pause which many of his audience did not notice but which was recognisable to anyone who had acted as a moment of pure terror.

"Praising the accursed thing." He finished and swiftly made his exit. For a moment Christ looked confused; it was not the right line. Then he recovered himself and spoke his own final words which Maltravers did not hear. Jackson had told him what the note to the Bishop had said. He also remembered the sergeant's remarks about coincidence.

Knowles was cleaning off his exaggerated make-up when Maltravers went up to him backstage.

"Don't tell me," said Knowles looking at Maltravers behind him in the mirror. "You of all people must have noticed."

"I'm afraid we did although a lot of people wouldn't have. You got out of it very well. But they obviously weren't the right lines."

Knowles rubbed a rough towel over his face. "No they weren't," he mumbled through it then pulled his face clear and examined it again in the glass. "It should have been 'Death triumphant then shall reign, Endless night and endless bane'. God knows what mental fail-safe device threw out what I actually said. I'm afraid the fact that we're amateurs showed up rather badly there."

"Don't let it worry you," said Maltravers. "The only actor who never forgot his lines was Harpo Marx."

Knowles grinned and Maltravers was again conscious of the fact that humour somehow amplified the inescapable wickedness of his features. The fact that Knowles had shown him the letter about Hibbert and the Latimer Mercy came unexpectedly back into his mind. Nothing had come of it but it could have diverted the police's attention. And there was no proof that the letter had been genuine. Certainly its allegations had been found to be untrue.

"Let's hope I don't do the same thing on Saturday night," Knowles added. "That really is my big scene, even though I lose."

Knowles's apparently spontaneous but disturbing ad lib nagged at Maltravers' mind as they drove back to Punt Yard where Jenny the babysitter said that David Jackson had called and asked that Maltravers should ring him at home.

"We can't get Sinclair's story to add up," Jackson said when he answered. "There's a couple of points you might be able to help us with. According to Sinclair, he hadn't seen Miss Porter for nearly a year but one of the people he saw when he was back here has shown us a picture of them both at a party two months ago for the opening of a new London nightclub called the Seventh Heaven. According to our informant, you were there as well. Can you remember it?"

"Oh, God, yes. Dreadful place. I only went there by chance

because I was mixed up with some crowd or other that evening. I can't recall much about it."

"Did you see Sinclair and Miss Porter there?"

"I remember talking briefly to Diana but she was with some other people. I can't remember seeing Sinclair but there were so many free-loaders and the usual riff-raff about I didn't take much notice. I only stayed about an hour and the place was packed out."

"Well, he certainly was there because he's in the picture so we'll have to ask him to explain that. The other thing is, do you know a Mark Kenyon?"

"Mark Kenyon? Yes, he's a freelance cameraman. Was he there as well?"

"He can't have been because he left the country a couple of weeks previously and still isn't back. He's working on some series or other in Australia. But we're told he was Diana's boyfriend and at least two people reckon he's the father of the child."

"They know more than I do," said Maltravers. "I told you that our lives drifted apart a great deal. Anyway it's more significant surely that Sinclair's lying."

"Yes. We've asked Los Angeles police to talk to him again. The problem is that his movements can only be confirmed up to the lunchtime of the Sunday Miss Porter disappeared. After that he says he was in the flat until his flight from Heathrow on the Wednesday. He claims he had eaten something that upset him at lunchtime on Sunday and was ill for two days.

"There's one other thing that makes me think. He spent that Sunday lunchtime in a wine bar off Shaftesbury Avenue and the man who met him there told us that they talked about Miss Porter's appearance at the festival. He remembers Sinclair saying 'Fancy dying on a Saturday night in Vercaster'.

"Now I know what that sort of remark means in the show business world but it's an odd thing to say when you think about what's happened, isn't it?"

Chapter 13

To MADDEN'S INTENSE annoyance, Powell's camping spot in Wales remained undiscovered. Reported sightings were marked on the incident room map with red pins, replaced with yellow when they had been checked; the land mass beyond Offa's Dyke took on the appearance of a pig with an unpleasant skin disorder. Madden's irritation was compounded by the news on Sinclair, having assumed inquiries in London would clear him. He read the report gloomily.

"After Sunday lunch, when he says he was at home being ill, he's not got a story we can substantiate?"

"No, sir. According to what he has told the Los Angeles police," Jackson glanced at the papers he was holding, "he went to another show on the Tuesday after he had recovered but, as on the Saturday, he says he was alone."

"Seventy-two hours he can't account for. That's quite a long time."

"And it happens to cover the most vital period, sir."

Madden looked at the report on Sinclair again with evident distaste. It was planting seeds of doubt in his mind which interfered with the smooth pattern that led to Arthur Powell.

"Do you want someone from here to go and see Sinclair, sir?" Jackson asked.

Madden shook his head vigorously, rebutting the suggestion and stamping on his doubts at the same time.

"I can see no justification for sending officers to California at the public expense on the strength of what we have so far. One chance return visit to England, some quarrel with Miss Porter a long time ago and a period he has no alibi for do not add up to a substantial case. Continue inquiries in London. Check with the theatres he says he visited. If he's an actor they may remember him being there. In the meantime the search for Arthur Powell continues."

The holes in Sinclair's story remained. The two shows he had been to see were among the most successful in the West End, drawing packed houses almost every night. The managers at both theatres were apologetic when the police called but it was impossible to remember who might have been there apart from the most well-known public faces. One produced a virtual Who's Who of names from the worlds of show business, politics and sport who had been his patrons but did not recognise Sinclair when shown his photograph.

"There are a great many minor actors," he said condescendingly. "There are members of the cast in this theatre I wouldn't know in the street."

In America Sinclair stuck to his story. He agreed he had been at the nightclub opening but could not remember seeing Diana there. He violently denied being specifically in her company. His remark in the wine bar was a casual comment without any meaning. He could offer no further information about his movements after Sunday lunchtime or suggest anyone who could vouch for him. The police report added that he was becoming increasingly agitated by their investigation and the producer of the television series had made a complaint about the interruptions their inquiries were causing. Jackson examined the nightclub photograph again. There were several people in the crowd between Sinclair and Diana and no indication that they were in fact together. So far the police had been able to contact only one person in the picture, a showbusiness hanger-on who did not know anybody or anything. They had been unable to establish even the names of several of the group grinning inanely at the camera.

The only line of inquiry remaining was to talk to Mark Kenyon, allegedly the father of Diana's baby, but he was not due back in London until early on Thursday morning. Two officers were detailed to meet his plane when it arrived at Heathrow.

On Wednesday Maltravers remembered the odd incident of what Knowles had said in the Mystery Plays; it had been driven out of his mind by the news concerning Peter Sinclair. He rang Jackson.

"I'll make a note of it," Jackson sighed patiently. "But unless you've got something useful like a motive don't expect us to do anything too drastic. You do realise, don't you, that we're in the middle of one of the biggest man-hunts this country has ever seen for a man we have every reason to suspect, is known to have been in Vercaster at the appropriate time and has now apparently vanished off the face of the earth? Plus this Sinclair business. Do you know how much sleep I've had in the last ten days?"

"I can make a guess. It's nothing more than an odd remark but I said I'd let you know anything that might be of use."

"Thank you." Jackson sounded very tired. "Find Arthur Powell. *That* will be of use."

Wednesday was market-day in Vercaster and it seemed that most of the population of the surrounding county was drawn to the city following some ancient impulse of race memory. The stalls appeared to sell unremarkable goods which could easily be purchased without the necessity of travelling several miles into the city and battling to find somewhere to park, but there was a sense of social occasion about the event.

Maltravers and Tess took Rebecca for a walk round as another way of passing the time. He was searching through some old books on one of the stalls in the faint hope of finding something of real value when Hibbert appeared through the door of the nearby Town Hall and saw him.

"Mr Maltravers," he said, crossing the cobbled space between them. "There's something I want to tell you. I've just been speaking to the Editor of the *Vercaster Times*. It will be in this week's edition." Hibbert paused pompously, leaving a dramatic moment before his announcement. "I have offered a reward for anyone giving information leading to the apprehension of Miss Porter's murderer. A thousand pounds." From Hibbert's entire demeanour, Maltravers realised that he anticipated effusive thanks for such benevolence. A thousand pounds, he reflected, was a substantial sum, excellently balanced between parsimony

145

and tasteless flamboyance. The credit accruing to Hibbert for such a gesture would make it money well spent.

"We're grateful for anything that will help sort this business out," he replied, dropping his response well below the level of gratitude Hibbert was hoping for.

"Yes," Hibbert continued slightly uncertainly when it was clear Maltravers was taking his thanks no further. "I imagine they'll be contacting you for some comment on the matter."

Maltravers noticed the Rotary badge glinting in Hibbert's lapel and wondered if the *Vercaster Times* Editor was also a member; he felt certain he was. Councillor Hibbert's offer would be handsomely reported.

"I imagine they will," he said evenly. The prospect of the insufferable Hibbert benefiting from Diana's horrendous fate was unspeakably offensive. Casually he indicated the box he had been looking through. "There might be something of interest to you here," he said mildly. "Although I think it's only their covers that are dirty. Good afternoon, Councillor." Hibbert watched him walk away with a look of bemused offence on his face.

A reporter from the *Vercaster Times* rang Maltravers at Punt Yard the following morning.

"Are you and Miss Davy staying in Vercaster until the end of the festival?" he asked.

"Personally, I'm staying here until Diana is found. This was the last place she was seen and I'm not leaving until we discover what happened to her."

"Obviously you're hoping she may still be alive?" Maltravers saw the angle he was looking for and gave him the reply he wanted.

"I don't care if the police say it's murder," he said. "Until I see Diana's body, I shall hold on to the belief that she may not be dead. We all know she's been terribly injured but there is no proof that she may not still be alive somewhere. However terrible the thought is, that's what is keeping us going." He could visualise the scribbling down of his eminently quotable comments but wondered bitterly if they had any real meaning or were just a continuing self-delusion. Did he really want Diana found, butchered like Lavinia but with a tongue to relate her torture?

146

"Thank you very much, Mr Maltravers," the reporter was saying. "We're checking with the police of course, but you don't know of any particular developments do you?"

"Nothing special. Do you know of anything?"

"No. There was some talk in the office about a reward yesterday but the Editor says it's not happening now."

"Really? Well, I don't think it would have been of much help at this stage." Maltravers had a feeling of satisfaction that his barbed remark to Hibbert had struck home.

One other thing was in fact happening, although nobody in Vercaster was aware of it. That morning an expensively dressed woman with raven black hair and a handsome, slightly hard face was thinking as she watched her children playing in the swimming pool in the garden of her home. She had just received a call from an actress friend in London who had casually mentioned the police interest in Peter Sinclair and his visit to England. She knew exactly what he had been doing from the Sunday lunchtime up to when he left to return to California. And she knew why he was lying about it.

When Mark Kenyon stepped off the plane from Sydney he was tired, jetlagged and had a streaming cold.

"What the hell's all this about?" he demanded when the police took him to an interview room. "I'm not smuggling anything."

"Do you know Miss Diana Porter, sir?"

"Di? Of course I do. Why?"

"I'm sorry to have to inform you sir, that Miss Porter has been missing for nearly two weeks and we have reason to believe that she may have been murdered."

Kenyon sneezed messily into a sodden mass of paper handkerchiefs. For a moment he sat catching his breath and looked at the officers with a mixture of weariness and bewilderment.

"What? Di murdered?" He shook his head as if to clear it then sneezed again. "When? Who by? Why are you talking to me?"

"Miss Porter was expecting a baby, sir. We have reason to believe you may have been the father."

Groping his way through a mental fog of infection and exhaustion, Kenyon began to comprehend what was being said to him.

147

"I didn't know that," he said. "But it's what was supposed to happen."

"When did you last see her?"

"The night before I went away. When was that? About ten weeks ago. She didn't say anything about it then."

"It's probable she didn't know at the time, sir. I'm afraid we'll have to ask you to give us a full statement about your relationship with Miss Porter."

Kenyon was overcome by another series of explosive sneezes. He fumbled in his pockets for a less useless wad of tissues.

"Look," he said as the paroxysm subsided. "Does this have to be now? I'm in no state to talk to anyone. Let me go home and get some sleep, then you can ask me anything. At the moment I can't even take in what you're saying to me." The two officers looked at each other. "For God's sake, I'm not going anywhere. But anything I say at the moment will be gibberish. I can hardly stay upright."

One officer nodded almost imperceptibly to the other.

"We have a car outside, sir." he said. "We can take you home."

Kenyon slumped in the back seat of the car and was asleep before they had left the airport. They roused him when they reached his house in Wimbledon and helped him out of the car as he fumbled for his keys.

"Look," he said as he opened the door. "Don't get me wrong but I just can't take in what you're saying. You said that Diana's been strangled?"

"We didn't actually say strangled, sir, because we don't know. But we do believe she's been murdered."

Kenyon rubbed his hand across his forehead. "Funny, I thought you said strangled. I can't think straight at the moment."

"Do you mind if we wait here while you have a rest, sir?"

"Do what the hell you want," Kenyon said, stumbling up the stairs. "As long as I get some sleep you can end the world for all I care. Just don't make too much noise."

While Kenyon slept, more inquiries were made with the television crew he had been working with. There was not the slightest possibility of him having left Australia in the previous ten weeks. His apparent lack of concern at the news of what had happened to Diana Porter and his reference to her having been strangled were put down to the state he was in on his arrival, until the police could question him further. He slept for nearly eight hours, then reappeared in the room where the two policemen were playing cards.

"You weren't a dream then?" he said. "Let me get a coffee and tell me all that again."

"I'll make it, sir," said one of the officers and went into the kitchen. The other picked up an envelope that was lying on the table.

"We saw this among your post, sir," he said. "It's not been tampered with in any way but it does appear to be a woman's handwriting. Can you say if it's Miss Porter's?"

Kenyon took the envelope and stared bleary eyed at it, then nodded.

"If you could open it, sir, it might be of assistance to us."

Kenyon sat down and blew his nose, then ripped open the flap of the envelope. The letter inside was written on one side of a single sheet of pale blue notepaper. He read it through then handed it across to the policeman without a word.

"Dear Mark," the note said. "I'll be away by the time you get back but I wanted you to know as soon as possible that it's been confirmed today that I'm pregnant. I'm very happy and very well and should be a mother by Christmas. I'll see you when I get back. All my love, Diana." It was dated four days after Kenyon had flown to Australia. The policeman looked inquiringly at him.

"She wanted to have a baby," he said in reply to the unspoken question. "But she didn't want a marriage. It's not altogether uncommon. I met her at a party and we liked each other very much. She was perfectly honest about it. Obviously she wanted to feel . . . some affection for the father but the baby would be hers. I accepted her terms." He pressed a handkerchief to his running nose. "That's all there is to it really. Now what the hell's all this about her being murdered?"

"You've not heard what's happened at all?"

"Not a thing. I've been somewhere in the outback of beyond most of the time."

The policeman told him of the events surrounding Vercaster. Kenyon listened unemotionally as he finished, then accepted the coffee brought through by the other officer.

"I'll probably react to all that later," he said. "It's a lot to take in all at once. I'm sorry I can't play the grief-stricken lover if that's what you expect. I was very fond of Diana but I'm not going to pretend I was madly in love with her. That wasn't part of our arrangement. But I can't see how I can help you."

"You said something earlier about her being strangled. We never said that."

"I knew you'd pick that up. You'll just have to believe me that I didn't know my own name when I got off that plane. I saw Diana about ten weeks ago and she was alive and well and that's how I left her. Don't try and pin a murder on me for some meaningless remark."

"There's just one thing you might be able to help with. Do you know a man called Peter Sinclair?"

"Sinclair?" Kenyon thought for a moment then it came back to him. "Oh, that prat. Depends what you mean by know him. We've been in the same studio. Why?"

"Did Miss Porter ever talk about him?"

"She talked about a lot of people. Let me think. They'd appeared in something together once she told me. What was it? No, it's gone . . . but we saw him once . . . where was it? That's it, it was a Variety Club Lunch for someone or other. He was sitting with . . . what's her name? . . . Vicky Price, that black-haired cow who quit acting a while back and married some smart Harley Street doctor. They were at a table on the other side of the room. Diana said something about him being the most evil man she'd ever known." Having pieced together the picture out of his memory, Kenyon suddenly saw the nature of it.

"Are you saying that he did it?" he exploded. "Why haven't you got him yet?"

"We have no evidence, sir, and in fact Mr Sinclair may well have an alibi. Do you know why Miss Porter said he was evil?"

"No. But I know she meant it. And Diana did not like disliking people." Suddenly he sneezed again.

"We'd like to take your statement now, sir."

150

The Variety Club Lunch had taken place three weeks before Kenyon went to Australia. Sinclair, who had claimed not to have seen Diana Porter for more than a year, was now known to have been twice in the same company within the previous four months and the long unfilled period of time remained in his visit.

Chapter 14

MADDEN SAT ALONE in his office on Friday morning and wrestled with the problem of the continuing absence of Powell and the lack of an adequate alibi for Sinclair. All his experience and instincts still centred on Powell, whose failure to come forward was tantamount to an admission of guilt. He found it unbelievable that Powell could not know the police were looking for him. Never before had Madden faced an inquiry in which the known facts stubbornly refused to fit a recognised pattern. While Maltravers might only dream of solving crimes, Madden knew from long experience how they should be investigated and settled, but the very discipline of proper inquiries, which had never failed before, was now a fatal handicap. At his centre, William Madden had one terrible human failing — he could not admit that he might be wrong.

It was now, he considered, only a matter of time before Powell was arrested and the lack of an alibi for Sinclair would become academic. But how long could he afford to wait before taking direct action on Sinclair? Forty-eight hours, he decided. Until then he would put these irrational misgivings down to overwork. Certainly for most of the previous fortnight no police officer in Britain had worked longer or more conscientiously in the hunt for Diana Porter and her killer.

Maltravers now had all his waking moments — and many of his sleeping ones — haunted by dread of inescapable abominations. He was finding it almost impossible to think clearly about everything that had happened in the now forlorn hope of identifying some key piece of information that would lead to the solution, however horrible it might be. More than anyone he wanted Diana to be found — dead or alive — and was quietly furious with his own impotence to do anything.

Grim faced, he walked again round the cathedral and the Chapter House. A note had been put on the case which had contained the Latimer Mercy explaining that it had been stolen and he gazed at it thoughtfully. It seemed an impossible length of time since he had first met David Jackson at that spot, when the only crime to be investigated was the esoteric theft of an old misprinted Bible. That was something he could have played with in his imagination, a pleasing intellectual exercise in which he might demonstrate the incisiveness of his analytical brain. Now his mind was stultified with grief, worry and anger. He paused by the organ and noticed his own face in the mirror which the organist used to watch the choirmaster; his features were chillingly like those of his father in the last dreadful weeks before he died. He sat in the Chapter House, trying to recall faces he had seen there on the night of Diana's performance. While he was wrapped in his thoughts someone quietly sat down beside him. It was Miss Targett.

"I've been here almost every day since . . ." She smiled at him apologetically. "I don't know why. Whenever I sit here and think about all the dreadful things that have happened, one phrase keeps coming to mind." She paused then quoted softly: "All shall be well and all shall be well and all manner of thing shall be well."

Maltravers looked slightly surprised. "T. S. Eliot," he said. Little Gidding would not have struck him as being Miss Targett's sort of poetry.

"Pardon?" she said. "Oh, no. Dame Julian of Norwich. I remember Miss Porter speaking those words on television. But I'm afraid I cannot see how things can possibly be well now."

Unlike the last time he had seen her, Miss Targett was now composed but Maltravers still acutely sensed that the little old lady, her life previously settled and secure within a framework of innocence, had been irreversibly affected by being brought into contact with violence and wickedness. Her understated sorrow was all the more potent for her aura of dismay. He stood up and offered her his arm.

"May I walk you home, Miss Targett?"

She smiled gratefully. "That would be very kind."

153

Miss Targett's cottage was the end of the terrace at the corner of the alleyway leading from opposite the north transept to the city centre. When they reached the door she invited him in but he said he had to return to Punt Yard.

"Please give my love to Miss Davy," she said. "Tell her that you are both in my thoughts a great deal. Oh, and how is your leg incidentally? You don't seem to be limping."

"No, it's much better, thank you." Maltravers looked at her slightly puzzled. "But how did you know about it?"

Miss Targett frowned to herself. "I can't recall who told me about it. I think it was Mr Knowles after morning service on Sunday. I assumed that everyone knew about it. They really will have to do something about Talbot's Tower I fear. Somebody could be seriously injured." She extended her small hand. "Thank you so much for seeing me home. God bless you."

As he walked back to Punt Yard, Maltravers met the Dean and Webster by the Lady Chapel.

"Still no news?" the Dean inquired. "Oh this is intolerable. Every day I fear there will be some further outrage. Oh, forgive me. Your concern can only be for Miss Porter. Is there still any hope that she . . ." He was unable to finish the sentence.

"I don't know," said Maltravers. "All I want now is for it to be over."

"It may not be much longer," said Webster. "All our prayers are with you."

The *Vercaster Times* was lying on the hall table when he went back into the house. Half the front page was given over to Diana's disappearance and the police hunt but there was no mention of Hibbert offering his reward. Maltravers' outraged offence in the market place two days earlier had given way to a pitying contempt for the vain, glory-seeking councillor and he wondered if he should have curbed his tongue. The offer of a reward would have done no harm, even though it seemed unlikely to have done any good.

There was a reception in the Town Hall that evening to which Maltravers and Tess had agreed to accompany Michael and Melissa. It had been planned as an occasion of thanks and congratulation on the eve of the final day of the festival but instead was a gathering of unrelieved tension. The Mayor made a speech, dutifully acknowledging the work that had gone into the event and touching on some of the highlights of the previous fortnight. Everyone listened in polite silence, many staring into their wine glasses, but his words had an inevitably hollow ring.

"Finally and most unhappily," he concluded, "I must express on behalf of everyone in Vercaster our sense of regret and horror at the dreadful events which have cast such a terrible shadow over all our endeavours. We have with us this evening some of the friends of Miss Diana Porter, whose performance in the Chapter House so magnificently launched our festival. We extend to them our deepest sympathies over the awful mystery of her disappearance and all that has happened since. We can only hope that even now Miss Porter may be found alive and the man who has perpetrated this wicked deed arrested."

The gathering coagulated into separate groups, each talking in hushed and uncomfortable tones. Maltravers was approached by a man he vaguely recognised who introduced himself as the producer of the Mystery Plays.

"I've seen you backstage but we haven't spoken," he said. "I'd just like you to know that we greatly appreciate your attending our performances. It can't have been easy for you."

"I've been grateful for something to do," said Maltravers. "And both Miss Davy and I have been very impressed by the standards you have achieved." He paused momentarily, then forced himself to add, "I'm sure Diana would have shared our opinion."

Slowly and inevitably he was beginning to think and speak about Diana in the past. He was the last one who would fully accept the fact of her death without absolute proof. The producer made no comment but smiled sympathetically and walked away.

Across the room Maltravers caught Hibbert's eye. The councillor immediately turned away and began talking in an unnaturally loud voice.

"Of course we mustn't lose sight of the fact that it has been an absolutely marvellous festival," he said. "Tremendous credit to Vercaster. Let's not forget that."

Several people turned and stared at him in disbelief but he was impervious to their looks. He walked across the room and started talking to the Mayor about how the event should become an annual occasion.

Tess gently squeezed Maltravers' arm as he glared at the obscene councillor.

"Ignore him," she said softly. "He's making a fool of himself."

"He's getting back at me," Maltravers replied. "He's a very nasty little man."

Hibbert's insensitive behaviour brought about the last thing he would have wished, the departure of his audience. There was a notable movement towards the exit in which a clearly embarrassed Mayor and Mayoress joined. They waited outside the door and spoke to Tess and Maltravers as they were leaving.

"It was very kind of you to come," said the Mayor. "I feel I should perhaps apologise for what happened in there just now. I don't understand it at all."

"I think I do, your Worship," Maltravers replied. "But it doesn't matter."

The Mayoress offered her cheek to Maltravers to say goodnight.

"I shouldn't say this," she whispered as their faces lightly touched, "but I've always thought Ernie Hibbert was a little turd." When she pulled her face away, it was that of a woman who would not know the word, let alone say it.

"You nearly made me smile then," Maltravers said. "That's not easy at the moment."

Over her shoulder he saw Jeremy Knowles give him a brief nod of farewell before leaving with other members of the Vercaster Players.

In the silent, late-night streets, as the four of them walked back to Punt Yard, workmen were erecting steel barriers along the route that the jousting knights and the rest of the medieval procession would follow to the fair the next day. They turned into the yard off the main road and saw a police car standing outside the house. Instinctively they quickened their steps and, as they approached, David Jackson stepped out.

"Your babysitter told me where you were and what time you'd be back. I couldn't see any necessity for disturbing you."

"Nothing dramatic then?" There was a note of disappointment in Maltravers' voice. Now any news was better than no news.

"Nothing dramatic. I'd just like another word about Sinclair."

He and Maltravers went into Michael's study and Tess brought them coffee.

"The more we test Sinclair's story, the more suspicious we get," Jackson said. "In fact, the problem is the big parts of it we can't test. We've got nearly three and a half days he can't or won't account for. He knows by now the way we're starting to think but he still can't produce any evidence to substantiate his story. Quite simply, if it isn't Powell then Mr Sinclair may find himself on his way back here much sooner than he expected."

He went over the details of Sinclair's story and the contradictions the police had uncovered.

"He may not be lying about not having seen Miss Porter for a year but it's not unreasonable to think he would have at least noticed her at one of the two events we now know they both attended. You knew her as well as anyone, better than most. Can you think of *anything* at all regarding Peter Sinclair? Mr Madden wants to give more time to tracing Powell before taking action, but I'm getting the feeling that somebody from here will be on their way to Los Angeles eventually. If you can think of some piece of evidence — or someone who might supply it — then possibly Mr Madden will act sooner."

"I've thought about it as much as any other aspect of this whole thing," Maltravers replied. "I've rung friends of hers that I know collect odd bits of gossip. If anything had come out I'd have told you. Do you think he's lying about what happened while he was here?"

"I don't think he's telling us the whole truth. The question is, what's he hiding?" Jackson sat in silence for a few moments staring into his coffee cup.

"The problem is that things have become so complex and extraordinary that we may have lost touch with some basics," he said finally. "You start any murder investigation by considering two simple things — motive and opportunity. In Powell's case motive is impossible to decide because God knows how his mind works. Opportunity is certainly there though. He was in

157

Vercaster and access into the Dean's garden through the trees at the bottom would have been simple. The same reasoning applies to Sinclair. Again an unknown motive but until we know where he was from Sunday lunchtime onwards we don't know that he was not here. A possible motive, of course, is jealousy. Was he the type to nurse a grudge after being rejected?"

"He's conceited, he's arrogant and he thinks he's God's gift to women," Maltravers replied. "But if all the men who think like that were homicidal maniacs you'd be very busy indeed. The problem remains as to why he should be attacking the Dean and the Bishop. And us of course."

"The same applies to Powell. But until we know what the motive is behind all this we're just guessing in the dark. The other thing about Sinclair that must not be overlooked is that he knew Miss Porter and most killers know their victims. Is he a good actor?"

"Not as good as he thinks but quite competent. Why?"

Jackson rubbed his eyes and yawned. "Oh, I was just thinking about knowledge of make-up and disguise, which he would know more about than most people. The fact that nobody saw him here doesn't necessarily mean much if you look at it that way."

Maltravers recalled Tess's successful imitation of a Yorkshire-woman in Belsthwaite. Sinclair did not have her talent but he could have enough to fool people who were not watching for him — and nobody had been watching for him. Odd, half-remembered faces from the reception in the Refectory floated into his mind and he wondered if they had all been what they appeared to be. The fact that Sinclair had opportunity was certain; whether or not he took it remained to be proved. Certainly Sinclair himself was doing nothing to refute it.

Jackson looked at his watch. "God, is that the time? I must get some sleep." He stood up and stretched. "Well at least the festival finishes tomorrow. It would be nice to think that every-thing else might finish as well."

158

Chapter 15

THE AFFLICTED VERCASTER festival was to end on the longest day of the year.

Early in the morning, rich with rising sunshine and the promise of a day of high summer, people began to filter onto the broad green slope of the cathedral meadow. The wide quietness was peppered with the sound of hammers as stalls were erected for the Medieval Fair and there was a growing murmur of voices. By the banks of the River Verta, flags hung limp and still around the jousting field for the mock tournament of the knights. From the refreshment marquee came the clatter of crockery and the chatter of attendants. In the middle of one open space a jester in chequered green and gold practised juggling with wooden balls, watched by a silent, fascinated little girl with her thumb in her mouth. Barrels of beer were tapped and the contents experimentally tasted. At the entrance to the fenced-off enclosure, a man fastidiously counted his float money.

Colour began to spread across the grass as the sounds of activity increased. Banners were erected, decorations put up, goods displayed. As the scene filled with more and more people, anticipation and excitement began slowly to grow. There was a burst of ribald laughter as a man grasped a girl dressed as Nell Gwynne from behind, squeezing her breasts, and she playfully slapped his face, her screams of pretended protest heard all over the field. On the top of Talbot's Tower a verger raised the standard of St George, then looked down through the battlements on the diminutive figures far below. A woman appeared holding a mass of helium-filled balloons, rising from her hand in the shape of a gigantic, multicoloured ice-cream cone. A bright green one slipped loose and soared swiftly into the clear sky to the shouts of delighted children.

*

Just after nine o'clock, the woman with the black hair saw her children off with the German au pair girl to go for their riding lesson. As she went back into the house the telephone rang and she answered it on the bedroom extension. The call was from Los Angeles.

"Peter, how lovely to hear from you! I was wondering when you'd call." The excessive sweetness of her voice was laced with bile. "I've been expecting to hear from you for ages."

"You know what's happened then?" Sinclair's voice was tense.

"The theatre grapevine's talking about nothing else, darling. Policemen popping up all over the place asking questions like *The Mousetrap* gone mad. Somebody was telling me they've even been talking to you."

"They've got good reason to, haven't they, although I've told them I haven't seen her during the last year."

"Oh come on, darling, there's no point in lying about that too, especially since someone's bound to talk."

"What do you mean?" Sinclair snapped.

"How about the Variety Club Lunch? *I* saw her there."

"You did? Well I didn't. I'm not lying about *that*."

"Oh, Peter," the woman said reproachfully. "I mean, I believe you, but do you really think the police are going to? Anyway, it probably doesn't matter because all the papers here are full of this man Powell. After all, he's the murderer, isn't he?"

"If they decide he's not, they're going to keep coming back to me. If you give me an alibi, then . . ."

"You listen to me, little boy!" The lacing of bile had suddenly spread to become the entire fabric of her tone. "You're not getting me mixed up in this. If you try that I'll stitch you up so tightly you'll never get out. Understand?"

"You bloody little . . ."

"Now, Peter, you really mustn't call me horrid names." The abrupt return of her former treacly tones sounded perversely sinister now. "I could make life very difficult for you."

Sinclair began to sound desperate. "But I've got no excuse for coming back! I've got no alibis, there are no witnesses. The police don't believe me!"

"And nobody else is going to either. I mean, the truth really can't come out, can it?"

"They keep asking me about Diana's pregnancy. I expect everyone knows about it by now."

"Oh, yes, that's been in all the papers. Of course, I never listen to salacious gossip — unless my husband happens to tell me some secret of the consulting room and, of course, I always keep that to myself . . . don't I."

"You couldn't wait to tell me."

"Well, sweetie, after all the things you've said about Diana I was sure you'd want to know her good news. I thought you'd want to send her a card or something."

A sudden thought occurred to her. "Of course, the police don't know that I told you about it right at the beginning. Now that's something they would be very interested in, isn't it."

"But you're not going to tell them, are you?"

"If you try to drag me in for the alibi you're so desperate for I might have no alternative, darling. So you're going to be a good boy and not make Auntie Vickie cross, aren't you? I'm *sure* you'll manage to think of some story they'll believe. Sleep well. 'Bye."

Smiling to herself, she rang off and ran her fingers softly across the top of the phone, thinking for a few moments. Then she turned the bedside radio on while she dressed.

"And if you're anywhere near Vercaster today, watch out for traffic diversions because of the Medieval Fair they're holding this afternoon," the disc jockey was saying. "Sounds like a lot of fun if you're thinking of going. Knights on horseback, side-shows, plenty of fun for the kids. And what a lovely day for it as well. Might even pop along myself. Now, with the time just approaching nine minutes past nine o'clock, here's Neil Sedaka." The woman sang along with the record.

The tangible air of unreality in Punt Yard was amplified by Rebecca, who had insisted she should put on her Little Bo-Peep fancy-dress costume as soon as she got out of bed. She paraded proudly around the house in poke bonnet, frilled skirt and leggings tied at the ankles, with her miniature crook decorated

161

with a blue satin ribbon. She sang the nursery rhyme endlessly in a piping, off-key treble, constantly breaking off to ask how long before the fair began.

Sitting in the lounge with Tess, Maltravers was becoming increasingly resentful of the growing carnival atmosphere outside. The sense of gaiety callously ignored the grim events which had hung about the city for so long and paid no respect to any thoughts of Diana. Suddenly and viciously he told Rebecca to shut up and the startled child ran crying to her mother.

"That was unforgivable," said Tess crossly. "Stop taking it out on her. Go and tell her you're sorry." Melissa looked up at him reproachfully as he entered the kitchen.

"I'm sorry, darling," he said to Rebecca who was hiding her face in her mother's lap. "Uncle Gus isn't feeling very well this morning. Come on, we'll see what's happening outside." She peeped at him uncertainly for a moment, then held out her hand in forgiveness.

On the front step they stopped and Rebecca crowed with amazement as a man went unsteadily by on stilts, his height exaggerated by long red and white striped trousers. He heard her and smiled and raised his ridiculously tall hat in greeting. Maltravers was pulling the door closed behind them when a man ran up and grabbed his arm. It was Arthur Powell.

For a moment Maltravers did not recognise him. It was not the face of the photograph. He had several days' growth of beard and tears were staining his cheeks. In one hand he held a silver crash helmet.

"Diana!" he cried. "She's not dead! Tell me she's not! She can't be!" His fingers dug deep and painfully into Maltravers' wrist. "Tell me it's not true! It's all lies in the papers!"

Passers-by, many dressed in medieval costumes, stared towards the sound of his shouting, indelibly Welsh voice. Maltravers became aware that Rebecca's tiny hand had tightened its grip on his.

"Go back to mummy, darling," he said without looking at her. The front door was still open and she scampered back into the house. Powell was still staring at him beseechingly.

162

"Is everything all right?" A man had crossed from the opposite side of Punt Yard to see what was happening.

"Pardon?" Maltravers finally found his own voice. "Yes. Yes. It's all right." He turned back to Powell. "I think you'd better come in."

As he stepped to one side to let the distraught man enter first, Tess appeared down the hall and stared at Powell in disbelief as Maltravers followed him in.

"Call Jackson," he told her, then led Powell through to the lounge as Tess dashed into the study. Powell collapsed into a chair and began to sob bitterly as Melissa rushed into the room, freezing as she saw him.

"Augustus!"

"Go back and stay with Rebecca. The police are on their way." At that moment, Jackson and two constables were bundling into a car, its siren erupting into a piercing wail as it lurched forward.

Maltravers sat down in front of Powell, who raised his grief-twisted face towards him. His voice had broken into a painful croak.

"She's all right, isn't she?" he pleaded. "Please say she's all right." His emotion racked him again and he began rocking backwards and forwards, moaning.

"Where have you been?" Maltravers asked gently. He felt no emotion, least of all anger, towards the shattered man before him.

"Camping. On holiday." Powell sniffed noisily. "In Wales and then by Wast Water." It was the bleakest and loneliest spot Maltravers knew in England.

"You didn't hear anything about what happened?"

Powell shook his head violently. "Nothing. It was only early this morning when I saw an old paper in a cafe. I keep myself to myself you see. Then I came straight here." He looked at Maltravers searchingly. "But it is true, isn't it?"

Maltravers nodded and Powell finally crumpled with a whimper, then began to repeat Diana's name over and over. Tess had come into the room and was kneeling by Maltravers. She reached across and touched Powell's hand.

"You didn't hurt her did you?" she asked softly.

163

"Hurt her!" Powell stared back in horror. "I would never have hurt her! Don't you see? I loved her! I loved . . ." Choking tears overcame him again as there was the sound of screeching car brakes outside, followed by an urgent pounding on the front door. Tess went and opened it.

"Where is he?" Jackson snapped at her. She pointed wordlessly towards the lounge and he ran to it, followed by the two policemen. The sight of Maltravers and Powell, quietly sitting facing each other in easy chairs, was not what he had expected.

"Are you Arthur Wynn Powell?" he demanded brusquely.

Powell raised his face in bewilderment and blankly nodded. Jackson leaned down and took hold of his elbow.

"Arthur Wynn Powell, I am an officer with the Vercaster constabulary and have reason to believe you may have been concerned in the abduction of Miss Diana Porter. I am arresting you on suspicion of this offence. You are not obliged to say anything unless you wish to do so, but what you say may be put in writing and given in evidence."

Powell swayed in the chair, then flopped forward as Maltravers moved to support him. Jackson tightened the grip on his arm and pulled him to his feet. He was as helpless and obedient as a child.

"Come along," he said and there was an unexpected note of compassion in his voice. As he turned to lead him away, Maltravers was staring at Powell's feet.

"Just a moment," he said, then turned to Tess. "I said there was something we found out in Belsthwaite. Look at his shoes." Everybody's eyes, including Powell's, swivelled downwards.

"They're made of plastic, aren't they?" Maltravers asked and Powell dumbly nodded. "Like the sandals the supermarket manager showed us. After we were told you were a strict vegetarian. In fact, you're a Vegan, aren't you? Of course you are." He sighed and stood up. "I'm sorry, David, but this isn't your murderer. A true Vegan will not knowingly have anything to do with the taking of life under any circumstances. They won't even wear leather." He looked at Powell. "I know you didn't kill Diana. I don't know who did, but it wasn't you."

Jackson handed the passive Powell to the two constables. "Wait in the car," he said, then watched as Powell was led away before turning to Maltravers. "You really believe he's innocent?"

"I'm bloody convinced of it. Madden won't want to believe it — perhaps you don't — and he may have some difficulty in producing an alibi. But look at him. He's a very sad, mixed-up human being. He told us he loved Diana and I know exactly what he meant. He worshipped her with the sort of obsessive passion which is very commonly directed towards the famous and the beautiful. She was his fantasy woman and he must have imagined himself doing all sorts of things with her. But in real life he would not have had the courage even to speak to her. Add that to his Vegan beliefs and he's simply not your murderer."

"None of that's hard evidence."

"Perhaps not." Maltravers lit a cigarette. "And he's almost certainly got no witnesses to prove where he's been the past couple of weeks. But don't try to tell me that pitiful little Welshman killed the woman he loved.

"It's none of my business to tell you your job," he added as Jackson was leaving, "but I hope you go easy on him. It wasn't his fault you wasted so much time."

As the door closed behind Jackson, Melissa and Rebecca came into the room from the kitchen. The little girl ran to Maltravers.

"Come on, Uncle Gus," she pleaded. "We're going to see the fair. You promised."

As the police interrogation of Arthur Powell began, his motorcycle and side-car, parked in Punt Yard, were collected by a police van and taken in to be examined for any signs that the vehicle had been used to carry any parts of Diana's body. Powell, numb and moving like a man in a trance, was taken to an interview room and formally cautioned again.

"Do you wish to say anything?" Inspector Ruth Barratt asked him. "You are not obliged to say anything unless you wish to do so, but whatever you say will be taken down in writing and may be given in evidence." The words seemed to make no impression on Powell, his eyes fixed unseeingly on the bare table top.

"Do you wish to have a solicitor present?" Powell silently shook his head, then after a few moments, quietly spoke.

"I'll tell you the truth of it." As a policewoman took shorthand notes, he spoke for twenty minutes, then was taken to the police station cells and given a meal while his statement was typed and taken to Madden. It fitted in with all Maltravers had said.

Powell had first become aware of Diana Porter through the nude photograph in the paper and had been captivated by the images — not only sexual ones — which it had conjured in his mind. The letter he had written to her was his own inept and immature way of trying to express himself; the knife he had referred to was just another object of his irrational affection. He had visited Vercaster because he wanted to see her in real life. As far as he was concerned she could have recited the telephone directory in the Chapter House and he would have been satisfied. He had waited in Punt Yard the following afternoon for another glimpse of her until he realised Maltravers had noticed him. After that he had simply gone on holiday.

For two weeks he had seen no newspapers and heard no radio, living his solitary existence in the emptiest places he could find, feeding his loneliness and rejection of human company with the recollection of having seen Diana Porter, the remote, untouchable and unthreatening substitute for a normal relationship. He had stayed on National Park land where he did not ask anyone's permission to camp and, although he remembered being seen by occasional hikers, there was no one who could prove where he had been. The shock of reading about what had happened led him instinctively to make his way back to Vercaster as quickly as he could, desperately hoping that someone in Punt Yard would deny it all.

He had no alibis, no witnesses to his movements. Quietly, relentlessly, constantly, he repeated his innocence of having harmed Diana Porter in any way. Finally he fell into a brooding silence, his mind filled with the darkest shadows and deep personal hatred of whoever it was who had destroyed his private goddess. He signed the statement in a hand that had scarcely developed from the precise and concentrated writing of a child.

Seeing two weeks of meticulous police work dissolve, Madden was furious and frustrated. The initial report from the examination of Powell's vehicle said there appeared to be no traces of blood or anything else incriminating. And saliva tests proved that

166

he had not sent the packages to the Dean and the Bishop. Madden gave orders for two officers to fly to Los Angeles, then stalked through to the incident room. Surrounded by files, maps, reports and other miscellaneous paraphernalia of the manhunt for Powell, his team listened in subdued and deflated silence.

"It appears possible, perhaps even likely, that hundreds of police hours and thousands of pounds of public money have been wasted." Madden glowered round the room as if he were holding everyone in it personally responsible for the situation. "Unless we can find some hard evidence that Arthur Powell is a very clever murderer indeed, we are left in the position that nearly two weeks after Miss Porter vanished we could be no nearer finding the person or persons responsible. I have been given the personal approval of the Chief Constable to strengthen this inquiry team, if necessary with officers from other forces. However hard you have been working up to now, I expect you to work twice as hard from now on. Inspector Barratt, Sergeant Jackson, Sergeant Neale — my office." With a final glare, Madden left the room and his audience visibly relaxed.

When Jackson and the others entered Madden's office he had his back to them, staring through the window at the passing traffic. They stood in an uncertain line waiting for him to speak.

"Arrange for Powell's story to be checked," he said without turning round. "He has told us where he claims to have been. Request the appropriate forces to see if they can find anyone who can substantiate his story." He slowly revolved to face them. "Within this room, I am not yet quite prepared to accept that we have been engaged on a monstrous and ridiculous wild-goose chase, though that is exactly what he may have caused."

Jackson wondered if Madden was actually contemplating some means of finding a way to charge the hapless Powell with wasting police time.

"If that is the case, however," Madden continued stonily, "we are left with only one other known suspect. This man Sinclair. While that is being investigated, there is one other avenue immediately open to us." He sat down.

"I want every available plain clothes officer at the Medieval

Fair this afternoon and the final performance of these Mystery Plays this evening. Everybody in Vercaster who has been in any way connected with this business will be there, particularly those most intimately connected with Miss Porter." He hesitated to let the significance of the remark sink in. He was returning to first, reliable principles that dictated that murderers almost invariably knew their victims.

"I am arranging to be on the official platform to watch the plays this evening. You may rest assured that I shall be as alert and on duty as anyone else. That is all."

Having realised that Powell could be slipping through his fingers, still convinced that Sinclair was an unlikely suspect, and faced with no other immediate possibilities, Madden was returning to one name that had never totally left his mind: that of Augustus Maltravers.

The cathedral meadow was now all noise, bustle, laughter, music and movement. Gleefully clutching a certificate, Little Bo-Peep ran across the grass to her parents.

"I won, mummy! I won!" She had in fact come second to a little boy dressed as Darth Vader who, Maltravers noted suspiciously, appeared to be the grandson of Councillor Hibbert, but any kind of award was a victory for Rebecca. From a loudspeaker on a pole near where they were standing a metallic voice announced that the knights were about to start jousting and they made their way down towards the riverside arena.

"I can't stop thinking about that sad little man," said Tess. "He's just another victim of all this."

"I wonder if Madden can see that," replied Maltravers.

They reached the edge of the roped-off enclosure in which a man was introducing the combatants, divided for maximum effect into the goodies and the baddies. They were led respectively by Sir Geoffrey of Leicester, with an air of suitably modest chivalry, and the aggressive and uncouth Black Knight, scowling as he was jeered by the crowd and then taking it out on his dwarfish squire with a gratuitous kick. Their attendant knights battled spectacularly in a skilfully rehearsed programme, then the two principals galloped thunderously towards each other.

The Black Knight was unseated and ran in fury to take an alarmingly real looking two-handed sword from the side of the arena and brandish it, bawling defiance at his shining opponent. Sir Geoffrey dismounted, armed himself with a matching weapon, and the crowd went quiet as the clang of heavy blades sounded across the arena. What had been a harmless piece of entertainment took on an unnerving air of genuine viciousness.

"They've got him I understand?" a voice said behind Maltravers' shoulder. It was Jeremy Knowles.

"Pardon? Oh, yes Powell. How did you know?"

"I had to go to the police station this morning. The son of a client was on a drugs offence. The place was full of the news. You must be very relieved."

"Not really." Maltravers stepped back from the rope so he could speak to Knowles more easily and started to explain.

"And you felt quite sure he was telling the truth?" Knowles interrupted.

"Absolutely. That man's no more guilty than you or I."

"That explains why Mr Madden was looking so ill-humoured when I saw him in the corridor. Where do they go from here?"

Their voices were drowned by a chorus of boos as the Black Knight perpetrated some further misdemeanour and they both turned to look. The opposing knights were galloping towards each other furiously, the banners that covered their horses flapping wildly. They were only a few yards apart when a giant of a man in a leather jerkin stepped imperiously between them holding a sword aloft and bellowed for them to halt. One horse reared violently, its flying hooves catching the glare of the sun before thudding down within inches of the referee.

"That was too close for comfort," said Knowles. "They usually leave a greater margin of safety than that."

"You've seen them before then?"

"Oh, yes, they're a popular attraction around here. My brother's the Black Knight. Of course it's all as arranged as a wrestling match — he has to lose at the end." He smiled sardonically. "Like me tonight."

Maltravers looked again at the Black Knight and now saw the family resemblance. When he turned back Jeremy Knowles was

169

walking hurriedly away. In the arena it was being announced that there would be a period while tempers were allowed to cool before a final melee.

For the remainder of the afternoon they wandered idly about the fair. Maltravers bought Tess a brooch shaped like Talbot's Tower from the cathedral stall.

"A souvenir of Vercaster," he said as he pinned it to her shirt.

"I've got a lot of those," she replied.

They were listening to the band from Vercaster's French twin-town playing beneath its tented awning, the musicians in deep shade amid the brilliant, hot sunshine, when Jackson walked up to them.

"Has Powell convinced Madden yet?" Maltravers asked him.

"Shall we say that Mr Madden has severe doubts? We're still waiting for anything from Wales or the Lake District that might prove his story. But I agree with you. I can't see that he did it." A uniformed policeman strolled by and studiously ignored him. "At the moment we're concentrating our efforts here. As Mr Madden says, all the principals are hereabouts. I've seen all the clergy and several other people who were at the performance in the Chapter House."

Maltravers looked round and saw the gaitered Dean approaching.

"Do you think there's a murderer among them?" he asked Jackson.

"There's a murderer somewhere." Jackson quietly stepped back into the crowd as the Dean reached them, grave and sympathetic.

"Our celebrations must be somewhat painful for you," he said.

"It's what my sister refers to as 'being British'." Maltravers gave the Dean a rueful smile. "You know that Powell's turned up?"

"Canon Cowan told me what happened this morning. It's ironic that what we supposed would resolve everything seems to have somehow made matters worse." The Dean seemed lost for anything further to say. With a smile for Tess he excused himself and walked away.

As the afternoon wore lazily on amid the colour and

cacophony, Maltravers twice saw Jackson, each time quietly talking to other people whom he supposed were plain clothes officers. He spotted occasional men and women in the crowd who seemed detached from their carnival surroundings, their eyes passing with unnatural keenness over people's faces; running through the Medieval Fair was a sharp edge of police activity.

Rebecca started to wilt as the novelty of everything began to pall and tiredness took over so they began to stroll back towards Punt Yard. They passed a gallery of raked seats that had been set up on a platform opposite a wooden stage on the south side of the Refectory.

"That's where we are tonight," said Melissa. "For the Mystery Plays. The seats are for the organising committee and invited guests. Everyone else sits on the grass." She looked at the empty seats and stage for a moment. "Then it's all over, thank God." Distantly, from the far end of the field, there was a roar as the good and bad knights began their final merciless combat.

When they returned in the early evening, the crowds had gone from the fair and the dusk-washed meadow was spread with its remnants. Boy Scouts were collecting litter, a collapsed marquee was a sprawl of crumpled canvas, stalls were being dismantled again. Everything stopped as the time approached for the plays to begin. The only activity was far off on the opposite bank of the Verta where a handful of people moved about the scaffolding on which were fixed the fireworks that would end everything.

There was a wide area between the platform bearing the seats and the stage which was filling with people finding spaces to sit on the grass. Maltravers and Tess took their seats immediately behind the Bishop and his wife. The Bishop turned to speak to them.

"I've heard what happened today," he said confidentially as they leaned forward. "I'm sorry."

There was a distinctly uneasy feeling about the gathering on the platform, sitting in an awkward silence in contrast to the chattering people on the grass below. As they waited for the performance to start, conversation became increasingly difficult.

"It's a great pity they could not arrange for the plays to be performed by members of the ancient guilds who originally put them on." The Bishop was doing his best to ease the strain everybody felt by talking to the Dean who sat on his left. "Noah's Flood was done by the Verta watermen of course and the carpenters did the Crucifixion which was an obvious irony. I can't remember all the others. The tanners did the Temptation, the weavers the Judgement and the glovers the Adoration of the Magi. Of course the difficulty would be finding sufficient numbers following those trades today. Who was it did the Creation? The bakers I think. That might have been possible to arrange."

Maltravers glanced around the seats which were now nearly all full. All the cathedral clergy had arrived and there were several other faces he was sure he had seen in the Chapter House and at the Dean's garden party. As his gaze passed over them, his eyes paused when he saw Madden towards the back, who gave him a barely courteous nod of acknowledgement. He looked down among the crowd on the grass and thought he could recognise Jackson but, like all the others, the figure had his back to him. The voices went silent as a spotlight, placed on the roof of the Refectory behind them, abruptly threw a pool of light onto the centre of the stage and the plays began.

Into the light, a crowd of about thirty robed men and women slowly moved in a tight group then parted to reveal Jeremy Knowles in their midst, his costume almost a caricature of the classic image of Satan with pointed tail, curved horns and trident. He crept to the front of the stage like a spider and peered slowly round all the audience, then swept his trident round in a slow arc embracing them all in a web of evil and smiled knowingly with satisfaction. He whirled and raised his arms aloft towards the group which had formed like a choir behind him, then monstrously conducted them to speak.

"Crucify Him!" they shouted in obedient unison. The Devil turned back and bowed to his audience, indicating the mastery he had achieved over Man.

The Vercaster Players, who had impressed Maltravers already, rose to even greater heights as they portrayed the final terrible events of Christian legend. Christ betrayed and abandoned, crying in despair from the Cross, then slumped and deflated in death before striding in triumph from the tomb. But there was still the Devil to pay.

The plain backcloth of the stage suddenly fell and coloured spotlights danced on painted flames in the midst of which Knowles was coiled like a serpent ready to strike. Between the two principals, a crowd of souls swayed in confusion, now tempted by the Devil's cunning, now sweeping back to Christ's promise. Finally, as Knowles's cajolery turned to threats, they gathered behind Christ, who raised his white robed arms to cast a long shadow that engulfed his enemy. Knowles became beserk, his voice now a shriek.

"Where is my power?" he screamed, then staggered backwards and collapsed. As every eye was rivetted upon him he lay writhing on the floor like a man consumed by a fit. Suddenly the ground gave under him — there was a sheet of canvas covering a hole in the stage — and he vanished down it to an explosion of noise and bursts of crimson and purple smoke out of which emerged the figure of God. It was the dawn of Doomsday.

Tess, who had been as enthralled as anyone by a piece of spectacular and imaginative theatre, felt Maltravers grip her hand fiercely. She turned to him and he was transfixed with a look of total shock.

"Christ Almighty!" he said. "Where the hell is he?"

He leapt to his feet, looked swiftly all around and then roughly barged past people between him and the steps leading down from the platform, ignoring cries of protest and outrage. Behind him Madden rose as well and onstage the man playing God looked uncertainly towards the commotion. Maltravers leapt down the steps in one bound, grimacing when pain shot back into his leg as he landed, then overcame it as he dashed towards the Chapter House and round back into Punt Yard. He hammered at the door which was opened by Jenny. Upstairs he could hear the disturbed Rebecca crying.

"Has anyone been here? Have you heard anything?" The urgency in his voice dumbfounded the girl who shook her head blankly.

"Damn him!" Maltravers looked helplessly round the yard.

"Don't open the door again," he ordered and raced back towards the south·transept.

His pounding footsteps echoed round the slype as he ran to the door leading into the Chapter House. He turned the handle and pushed violently but it was locked. He went back through the silent cloisters and burst into the south aisle of the cathedral itself, the massive vaulted nave empty and hollow as he looked desperately around, panting for breath. In the turmoil of his mind he now knew there was no logic in his search. There was nobody in sight as he sped through the nave and out of the west door, stopping at the top of the cathedral steps. Impatience and frustration were feeding his rage as he surveyed the emptiness outside. He was about to run back to where the plays were continuing when he heard a creaking sound behind him. On one side of the porch was the door leading to the top of Talbot's Tower. Normally it was kept locked, now it shifted slightly on its ancient hinges.

He scrambled up the narrow staircase that corkscrewed through the stonework, his shoulders spasmodically bumping against the walls. The steps had deep concave impressions worn by centuries of use and several times he stumbled, swearing. He passed the point where a small plaque marked the spot where Bishop Talbot had collapsed and died. At the top of the steps was a low wooden arched door with a latch operated by a ring of rusty twisted iron. He grabbed it and turned, then hurled the door open and stepped, gasping for breath, onto the wooden platform which capped the top of Talbot's Tower.

From the rope of the flagpole in the centre hung Diana's head, tied by its long hair. On the opposite side of the battlements a figure crouched in a crenellation with its back to him.

"You evil bastard!" Maltravers forced the shout from his aching lungs.

Matthew Webster turned his head, his face livid with madness and fury.

"Evil?" he shrieked back. His arm shot out and pointed a quivering finger accusingly at Diana's head. "She was evil! She mocked God in His own house and spoke the words of your blasphemy!"

Maltravers slumped against the side of the door as a great weariness overcame him. He felt sick. For a long moment the two men looked at each other across the twenty feet between them.

"Give yourself up," said Maltravers. He pushed himself upright and stepped slowly towards the flagpole, an immense sadness on his face. Webster gave him a final look of total vindictiveness and was gone. Maltravers leapt across to the edge of the tower and looked down to see him crash face upwards onto one of the flying buttresses on the north side and heard the crack as his back broke. For a few seconds his body lay there like a rag doll, then slowly slid down the incline of the buttress to the ground. Maltravers heard a scream from behind him. Tess was standing in the doorway, her face frozen in horror at what she saw. As he crossed to her she wrenched her eyes away and clasped her hands over them. He took her in his arms and gently stroked her hair.

"It's all right," he said quietly. "It's all over now."

Below them the Mystery Plays had ended and five hundred voices began joyfully to sing Blake's *Jerusalem*. Across the Verta came the crackle of igniting fireworks and three great rockets streaked upwards to explode in white chrysanthemums of light.

"Go on down." Maltravers turned Tess so she could not see the flagpole. "I'll follow you in a moment." She stepped back through the door and began slowly to descend the stairs.

Maltravers untied Diana's hair then carefully wrapped her head in his jacket. As he turned to follow Tess a piece of stone with a flint embedded in it about the size of a tennis ball caught his eye. He picked it up and took it down with him. Halfway he met Jackson who looked at his face, then turned back without a word. In the porch Maltravers handed the jacket to the sergeant.

"Don't open it here," he said. "Where's Tess?"

"She went into the cathedral. What's that?"

Maltravers glanced at the piece of stone he was holding, then went to where the fallen masonry from the tower was kept. The piece that had hit him was on top. He looked at it, turned it over, then placed the piece he was holding into a gap in its edge.

"You were asking me about this when something interrupted us," he said. "He tried to kill me as well."

175

As Maltravers entered the nave, Tess was a lonely bowed figure sitting on a chair by the aisle. He walked softly up and sat down next to her. She was holding in her fingers the Talbot's Tower brooch, which she had unpinned from her shirt, savagely bending it backwards and forwards. It suddenly snapped in two. She gazed at the pieces for a moment then buried her head in Maltravers' shoulder as he put his arm round her. The silent building was filled with the sound of her sobbing.

Chapter 16

ON THE TOP floor of Matthew Webster's home was a small locked room, inside which the police found the mutilated remains of Diana Porter. Pinned to her dress was another typewritten Biblical text, this time from Exodus Chapter 22, Verse 18: "Thou shalt not suffer a witch to live". By the body was a meat cleaver on the wooden handle of which were found traces of her blood.

On the table by Webster's bed, along with his Bible and a book on the Revelation of St John the Divine, was his diary. The entry for the Sunday on which Diana disappeared read: "The woman is dead. Thanks be to God in whose eyes His servant is obedient." The only other entries were for appointments connected with his work or the festival. At the end of the garden which, like the adjacent Dean's, was thick with trees, police found a ready-dug shallow grave. The awful picture was completed with swift and sudden finality.

"There is only one matter which we may still need to investigate," said Madden. His eyes flickered across the attentive faces of Barratt and Jackson. "Did Webster actually jump off the tower? There were no independent witnesses as to what happened."

"Mr Maltravers is quite emphatic in his statement," Barratt replied. "He assumed that Webster thought he was going to attack him. He knew he was caught without any means of escape so he decided to take his own life."

"When Mr Maltravers suddenly . . ." Madden paused, then spoke the next words contemptuously, "solved the crime, he immediately decided to take matters into his own hands instead of informing the police."

"He saw that Webster had gone and was anxious to find him

before he could do whatever he was planning and get away with it. He said there was no time to explain his suspicions and if we had just discovered Miss Porter's head on the flagpole we might never have found who did it."

"You believe this . . . somewhat fanciful explanation of how he suddenly realised it was Webster?"

"He was right, sir. I'm sure he had not deliberately kept anything from us. He was more anxious than anyone that Miss Porter should be found. He feels guilty that he didn't realise the truth sooner."

Madden made no comment. Every aspect of the case annoyed him. The pointless manhunt for Powell, the wasted cost of sending two men to Los Angeles to question Sinclair, the massive police operation which had achieved nothing. And finally the solution coming from the one man who had never left his mind as a suspect. His mind was tormented by not knowing what happened on the top of Talbot's Tower.

"A report will be sent to the Director of Public Prosecutions," he said. "He will decide if further action is necessary. All officers to return to normal duties."

In the incident room a policewoman was methodically plucking the coloured pins marking reported sightings of Arthur Powell from the map of Britain and carefully dropping them into small cardboard boxes.

In Los Angeles, Peter Sinclair, who had been told that two police officers were flying from England to talk to him, received a phone call saying the interview had been cancelled because Diana's murderer had been found. He immediately made a transatlantic call.

"Just to let you know, sweetie, that they've found whoever it was," he said when the woman answered. "So now I don't need an alibi and I'm going to let everyone know what I was really doing. You can lie through your teeth now but I'll make damned sure your husband gets the message that you screw around."

The line went abruptly dead and she stood holding the receiver as her husband entered the room.

"Who was that?" he asked.

"Wrong number."

*

His face drained and grey, the Bishop looked an old and fragile man. He personally opened the door to Maltravers and Tess as they arrived at the Palace following his request to see them before they left Vercaster. He took them through to the lounge where his wife served coffee. Maltravers traced the floral pattern of the easy chair with his finger as the Bishop spoke.

"There is nothing I can say, except that we share your grief. I wanted to tell you that again before you left us. Matthew was a tortured and unbalanced young man but none of us realised it. I am very conscious of the fact that it was I who brought him to this cathedral." There was an uncomfortable silence which the Bishop finally broke himself. "I'm still not altogether clear as to how you finally realised it was him."

Maltravers sat forward in the chair, his coffee held in both hands.

"One odd thing triggered it all and at that instant I saw everything. I've had to consciously piece it together again since and what appals me most is that I knew so much but didn't realise sooner. Perhaps if I had . . ."

"Mr Maltravers you must not reproach yourself," the Bishop interrupted. "What did you know?"

"I expect it started right at the beginning. The first thing I was told about Matthew Webster was that he was zealous, over religious. It seems blindingly obvious now what the effect of Diana's performance would be on such a person. I had written it to stimulate, to put accepted beliefs in a different light. He was appalled by it and the fact that it was performed in the Chapter House made it more offensive to him. Then, to make matters worse, he saw people like yourself and the Dean congratulating Diana and me afterwards, praising what he could only see as blasphemy.

"The process was repeated at the Dean's garden party the following afternoon, everyone congratulating her again. It's fairly clear what must have happened. He went back to his own house next door and must have called Diana to the fence from his own garden when he saw her standing alone after most of the other guests had left. Whatever happened then would have been hidden by the bushes but they found a wound on her head indicating that she had been struck." The Bishop closed his eyes as if in pain.

"By now he was seeing himself as God's instrument of revenge," Maltravers went on. "That was the phrase he used to us when we were talking about the hunt for Powell. He had killed Diana but other people had to suffer. We were the next when he nailed her hand to the door in Punt Yard."

"But how could he have done that?" objected the Bishop. "That is one thing I cannot see. The Dean told me that he and his wife walked with Matthew from Cathedral Close and met you on the way to the cathedral. For the entire evening Matthew was at the organ and there was no interval. He came straight back into the nave at the end and you all left together."

"The first point is that nobody could see him from the nave," explained Maltravers. "His communication with the conductor was through the television camera. There wasn't an interval but the soloists sang the piece from Stainer's *Crucifixion* unaccompanied. I've timed it since on a recording Michael has and it lasts just about three minutes. That would have been time for him to leave the organ and go out through the door in the Lady Chapel on the south side. I used it myself once and it's directly opposite the front door of Michael and Melissa's house. The nail holding the hand was not hammered home. It wasn't so much a case of him not wanting to make too much noise, it was that he had time for only one quick blow before going back. There was no audience in the transepts or anywhere behind the choir screen so the chances of him being seen were minimal.

"One other thing is that when we met him on our way to the cathedral he was carrying a music case. Melissa remarked that she thought he would have known what he was going to play by heart. Diana's hand and the hammer and nail were in that case; the police have found bloodstains on the inside. Sending the other hand and the hair through the post was no difficulty. It only takes about half an hour to reach North London by car."

Despite his grief and shock, the Bishop was becoming interested in Maltravers' explanation.

"You said you knew other things?"

"One thing that seemed totally irrelevant at the time but which now appears significant is the conversation I had with him about misprinted Bibles. I was making a joke of it all but he said something about such things being regrettable as it was the word of God. I let it go out of my mind at the time but it was another indication of his narrow views."

"Are you saying he also took the Latimer Mercy?"

Maltravers shrugged. "There's no sign of it in his house but it's the obvious conclusion. Its presence in the cathedral — remember it was kept near the organ where he would frequently have seen it — would have been offensive to him. Perhaps the approaching festival and the fact that even more people than usual would see it made him do something. That must have been the start of it all. One thing that Jackson and I discussed more than once was the possibility of a link between the Latimer Mercy theft and Diana, but we couldn't see one."

"Do you think he destroyed it?"

"I'm not sure. He'd have had to balance the fact that it was misprinted against the fact that it was a Bible. I don't think any of us could understand how his mind worked so we can't know what he would have decided." Maltravers finished his coffee and carefully placed the cup and saucer on the table beside him. "It doesn't matter anyway. What does matter is that at one point he gave himself away and I didn't see it."

"Neither did I, nor Michael," Tess said quietly. "And you were in no state to notice things." The Bishop looked quizzically from one to the other.

"Tess is talking about the day he tried to kill me with a lump of masonry he threw off Talbot's Tower," said Maltravers. "The piece I found on top of the tower on Saturday night must have broken off as he pushed it over. We came up to the cathedral from Hibbert's Park and we would have been clearly visible from some distance away. He must have seen us approaching, grabbed one of the collection of pieces that had fallen previously — the one he chose isn't as heavy as it looks — and taken it up to the top. After throwing it at me he went down the tower staircase and back into the cathedral relying on the obvious fuss outside to give him cover. He then must have gone out of the north transept and along the alleyway that leads to the town centre.

"The people in the shop where he bought the violin strings say they remember he spent quite a while in there and drew particular attention to the time. It would have been an alibi if he needed it. He then walked back round the other way to enter Punt Yard from the main road end. I think he might have been planning to call at Michael and Melissa's house on some pretext and make a point of saying he was on his way back from the shop. In fact, he coincidentally met Michael on the way.

"The mistake he made — and got away with — was when Michael told him to go and investigate the fallen stone." Maltravers paused. "He never asked where it had happened. It could have been any one of three sides of the tower and how could he have known which one?"

"You're making him sound a very callous and deliberate murderer," the Bishop remarked. "I regard him more as an irrational young man. Would he really have been so calculating?"

"He had a sense of mission. He was carrying out what he saw as the will of God. I find that so irrational and self-deluding in the light of what he did that I think cunning would have been a part of it.

"The only thing that seems out of character is that he used Talbot's Tower at the end, although it occurred to me that technically the extension might not actually be consecrated. Bishop Talbot died on his way up to perform the service."

The Bishop shook his head. "No. That service would have been one of dedication and acceptance of the extension. Perhaps it was never carried out later but the land on which all parts of the cathedral stands is consecrated and nothing can alter that."

"I wonder if Webster realised that?" said Maltravers. "It seems that the tower would have served his purpose as the final act of vengeance on as many people as possible who had approved of what happened in the Chapter House. He was obviously going to haul the rope up and horrify them with the sight. The man had turned evil with madness." He was about to add more but Tess shot him a warning glance and he remained silent about the awful things men did in the name of a carpenter's gentle and mysterious son.

"There is a particular matter I wish to raise," the Bishop said after a pause. "The Dean has made the suggestion and I said I would ask you. If there are no objections from her family, it would . . . give us some comfort if Miss Porter were to be buried in the cathedral precincts. I don't know how you both feel about it."

Maltravers' emotional reaction was too confused for him to reply but Tess spoke for them both.

"Diana was entranced by your Chapter House and gave her greatest performance there," she said. "Whatever we may feel, I think she would have wanted it. It's very kind of . . ." Her voice suddenly broke on a hiccup of emotion and her hand flew to her mouth. "Excuse me. I'm sorry." She stood up and walked swiftly from the room, followed by the Bishop's wife. The Bishop, half risen from his seat, sadly watched the door close.

"I feared the suggestion might cause you distress," he said apologetically. "It's just that we feel a sense of responsibility and want to . . . I'm sure you understand." Maltravers nodded.

"There's only one other matter," the Bishop added. "At the start of our conversation you said there was something odd which — what was your phrase? — triggered it all in your mind."

"Oh, my Road to Damascus at the Mystery Plays." Maltravers gave a curious smile. "It was something you said, Bishop."

The Bishop's eyebrows went up. "Something *I* said? I remember trying to make some sort of conversation with the Dean because the atmosphere was so painful, but I can recall nothing of significance or even relevance."

"You were talking about the ancient craft guilds which traditionally performed the plays. Among others you referred to the Judgement — and that is important — and said it was done by the weavers. Just as the plays were ending, I remembered that the old name for the weavers was the websters." Maltravers held out his hands in a gesture of comprehension.

The Bishop shook his head sorrowfully. "His mind must have become very strange indeed to take that for a sign. We must go and find my wife and Miss Davy."

The Bishop's wife was sitting with Tess in the hall, holding her hand comfortingly. Tess went to the Bishop and took his hand, blinking tear-reddened eyes.

"I'm sorry to react like I did," she said. "It's a gesture Augustus and I appreciate very much. Thank you."

The Bishop kept her hand in his as they walked to the front door. Maltravers and Tess paused on the step to say goodbye.

"Whatever dreadful things afflict people," the Bishop said, "a clergyman can usually find something in the Bible that will bring some manner of comfort." His wife had gently taken his arm as his eyes turned to look straight into Maltravers'. "I shall pray for you both. And for Diana. And for Matthew."

Tess turned and walked down the path to stand by the front gate as the two men regarded each other in silence. Then Maltravers lowered his head slightly.

"Thank you," he said.

Tess's hands were gripping the black wrought-iron top of the gate as he reached her and she was staring at the cathedral opposite.

"Isn't it terrible when kindliness can hurt so much?" she said. As they walked back to Punt Yard, the clock in Talbot's Tower boomed the hour over Vercaster.

Two weeks later, the remains of Diana Porter were buried within the cathedral cloisters beneath a small, flat, marble stone bearing her name, the year she was born, the year she died and the single word "Actress". An inquest into the death of Matthew Webster recorded a verdict of suicide while the balance of mind was disturbed. His body was cremated and, at his parents' request, his ashes scattered on the waters of the River Verta. Three months afterwards, Arthur Powell hanged himself in his flat; the burnt remains of Diana's pictures were found in the grate. When the cathedral organ was renovated, the Latimer Mercy was found inside, wrapped in newspaper. It is no longer on display. The Vercaster festival was never held again.

SLEEPING IN THE BLOOD

'Maltravers returns to hackery to write a feature on
Sixties icon Jenni Hilton, re-emerged after 20 years'
obscurity . . . Gus's journalistic inquiries reawaken
old passions and fuel new, homicidal ones. Tense,
well-written, wickedly accurate on modern ad-world
and Sixties foibles' – *The Times*
0 575 05319 4   £3.99 net

Forthcoming Title

THE LAZARUS TREE

'Ancient Devon village, steeped in superstition,
scene of the murder of lecherous poet, harbours an
errant rector, a peeper, and a married teacher
(worried about his secretive teenage stepdaughter)
who has sent for Maltravers to help out . . .
Richardson in sombre vein, fermenting a rich, heady
brew of past indiscretions, present revelations' –
Sunday Times
0 575 05522 7   £4.50 net